ANOTHER PLACE YOU'VE NEVER BEEN

ANOTHER PLACE YOU'VE NEVER BEEN

A Novel

REBECCA KAUFFMAN

COUNTERPOINT | BERKELEY, CALIFORNIA

The Library of Congress has cataloged the hardcover edition as follows:
Names: Kauffman, Rebecca, author.
Title: Another place you've never been : a novel / Rebecca Kauffman.
Description: Berkeley : Soft Skull Press, an imprint of Counterpoint Press, [2016]
Identifiers: LCCN 2016020217 | ISBN 9781593766566 (hardback)
Subjects: LCSH: Women—Fiction. | Fate and fatalism—Fiction. | Buffalo (N.Y.)—Fiction. | BISAC: FICTION / Literary.
Classification: LCC PS3611.A82325 A56 2016 | DDC 813/.6—dc23
LC record available at https://lccn.loc.gov/2016020217

Cover design by Kelly Winton
Interior design by Elyse Strongin, Neuwirth & Associates

Paperback ISBN: 978-1-64009-007-1

Counterpoint Press
2560 Ninth Street, Suite 318
Berkeley, CA 94710
www.counterpointpress.com

Printed in the United States of America

To my Mama, Daddy, and Sis,
with all my love.

CONTENTS

ANOTHER
PLACE
YOU'VE
NEVER
BEEN

PROLOGUE

A THOUSAND VOICES

The North Dakota plain was as flat and yellow as a cornmeal pancake, dotted with small gleaming ranch homes and dusty vehicles. The reservation was too quiet and too hot. It was August.

Two brothers went to a swimming hole. The Older Brother rode their bicycle, and the Younger Brother balanced on the handlebars. The swimming hole was several miles from their home, a single-wide periwinkle trailer that sat at the easternmost border of Sunflower Gates motor home park. The brothers rode past the sprawling wheat mill and processing plant that overlooked Sunflower Gates, and into town. Past the St. Francis mission, the IGA, Twin Bear liquor store, the tire place on Thief River Road, and their cousin Sonny's home, where his girlfriend sipped an orange soda and waved to them from the porch. They rode past fields of wheat and hay and sugar beets. When they reached the swimming hole, they took all of their clothing off and hung it in the branches of a white willow tree. Their bodies were sun-browned, their hair gleaming like black liquid gold.

The Younger Brother sang loudly, and beautifully.

The water was warm and thin and dark. The brothers somersaulted and grabbed at frogs in the shallow end. They dove into the deep end from a bouncing piece of oak that jutted out from a small, groaning wooden platform. They tossed handfuls of pond muck at one another. The Older Brother noticed a school of mid-sized bluegills, and he left the water to retrieve the long-handled net they had brought for this purpose. When he returned to the pond, he didn't see the Younger Brother.

The Older Brother walked along the edge of the pond, through crisp reeds and tall cattails whose fluffy innards oozed from their pods. He gazed out across the far side of the pond to see if his brother had perhaps gotten out and dried off. He watched the surface of the water for bubbles or a series of circles that would indicate his brother's whereabouts. He had always worried about the Younger Brother, who was reckless and unafraid.

He called the Younger Brother's name.

Finally, the Younger Brother burst from the water's surface at the far end of the pond, the deep end, and he was gasping. He swam frantically and with poor form to the edge of the pond, where he scrambled out. The Older Brother ran to him. The Younger Brother sat and coughed and coughed. The Older Brother sat with him.

The Younger Brother examined his feet and ankles, which were speckled with tiny spots of red. He said, "Don't go back in the water."

The Older Brother said, "What's down there?" He was very afraid.

"Barbed wire." The Younger Brother rose and said, "Let's go home."

The Younger Brother said he'd like to ride the bicycle home, reminding the Older Brother that it was his turn, and insisting that he was fine. Before mounting the bicycle, the Younger Brother ran his T-shirt over his feet and ankles, which were still bleeding slowly but steadily, and appeared a bit swollen. The Older Brother climbed onto the handlebars of the bike.

They hadn't yet reached town when the front wheel of the bike took a sharp turn, waggling first, then nosing directly into the ground, and the Older Brother stumbled headfirst onto the shoulder of the dirt road. The Older Brother leapt to his feet and went to his Younger Brother, who now lay quietly at the side of the road with the bicycle still between his legs. The Older Brother shook the Younger Brother's shoulder and said his name over and over, but the Younger Brother was cold and dead.

The men of the community drained the pond the next day, and where the Younger Brother had been tangled beneath the surface, they found not barbed wire, but a nest of venomous water moccasin snakes. This breed was thought to live exclusively in the Southeast—never before had a sighting been reported north of the state of Virginia. Perplexed and aggrieved, the men used shovels and hoes to chop the snakes to pieces, the bloody black parts wriggling in the dry grass long after their heads had been removed.

• • •

The Older Brother lived to be elderly, and when he died, he was buried next to the Younger Brother in Grandfather Tree Cemetery, beneath the white willows. On the day of his burial, after the crowd had dispersed, several astonished onlookers reported a sighting of the Younger Brother at his grave. And although he was recognizable for his strong features and resemblance to the Older Brother, the Younger Brother had grown huge, aged, and transformed to a Two-Spirit in the Underworld, witnesses claimed; for now he had the appearance of a female.

The Two-Spirit quickly disappeared into the high grass of the wheat fields that day, but over time, reports from various locations corroborated this sighting. Elders collected these accounts and shared them with one another in attempts to identify his/her patterns and purpose. The Two-Spirit appeared as a female to some and a male to others, and it was not clear whether this was the result of any actual sort of transformation, or if it was simply a difference in the perception of the observer. It seemed that oftentimes, but not always, the Two-Spirit appeared to those for whom Death was near, and they believed that the Two-Spirit had healing powers, but did not always choose to use them. They said that people feared the Two-Spirit, although no one knew of any violence he/she had committed. He/she often traveled alongside water, they noted, and they speculated that perhaps he/she passed to and from the Underworld by way of the sea.

Many years later, young Ojibwa children ask the elders about the strange dry pit carved from the North Dakota plain, out beyond the wheat and hay and sugar beet fields, where there are still remains of the diving board platform at the east end, splintered oak with stray rusted nails. Within the pit, there can be found a half-buried shoe, some fishing line, a flat, floppy basketball yellowed by the sun.

The elders tell them the story of the brothers. Unlike the stories they're accustomed to being told, the children don't know what to make of this one. Oftentimes, they will go home and ask their parents to retell the story. Then the children will retell the story to one another. They feel something different in each retelling. They are learning that sometimes it takes a thousand voices to tell one story.

ME OR THE MOUSE

Marty was going on for the fifth time that day about how they'd have to cool it with the hard liquor once his daughter arrived. She was only ten years old but she wasn't some clueless idiot, he said, and he didn't want her reporting back to her mother that he was boozing and crashing all summer long. Besides, he was really hurting for cash, he continued, come to think of it, April hadn't paid for a thing in months. Not a single Q-tip. Not one slice of cheese.

"OK, chief," April said. She was working an emery board over her thumbnail. Her little white Tupperware basket full of manicure supplies sat on the coffee table in front of her. She finished with the file and ran her fingers through the white basket, the small glass bottles of polish clicking against one another like dice.

She settled on navy with silver glitter and smacked the bottle against her palm before starting to apply it.

"Love that shade, babe," Marty said from the La-Z-Boy. He pulled hard and noisy on his cigarette before exhaling, using his lips to direct it at a sharp angle toward the open window. Marty had soft, thick lips and nice eyes, but teeth that were splayed out like they'd been hit hard from the inside. April was out of his league, looks-wise, but Marty was a real decent guy. He gave her a hard time about money sometimes, but he was never serious.

The armrests of his La-Z-Boy were worn to strings, exposing bulges of mustard-colored stuffing, which he pinched absently. He wore a camouflage baseball cap over knotty shoulder-length hair.

"Did you remember to get them air freshener things?" he said.

April nodded toward the plastic bag at the foot of the couch.

"Did you get different flavors?"

"Mm-hm." She didn't look up from her nails.

"Babe?" he said.

"*Yes*, I got friggin' vanilla, ocean mist, mountain something or other."

Marty was so annoying lately. Ever since it had been decided that his daughter would spend the summer with him, he'd been on his high horse about getting the place clean, sobering up, smoking out the window, color-coded trash bins. He'd spent the last month trying to convince April that this would be good for the two of them too; getting their act together a little bit, healthier lifestyle, looking after a kid, et cetera. Not likely, April thought. She wasn't much for recycling, et cetera.

April finished her nails and went to the kitchen. She tossed two burritos wrapped in foil onto a baking sheet and turned on the oven. She stared at her reflection in the toaster while the oven ticked and hummed like it was changing gears. She ran her fingers tight through her bangs to check the status of her roots. She bleached her hair every three weeks to keep it white-blond, and blow-dried it upside down every morning, then made it even bigger with mousse and a wide-tooth comb. Even with all that volume, it fell past her shoulder blades. She had a great head of hair, people said so all the time. She hadn't had it short since the first grade.

She brushed some cigarette ash from her thighs. She was wearing denim capris and a denim snap-up shirt. She was also wearing her white vinyl high heels and they were sexy as hell, even with the bright green grass scuffs that crisscrossed the sides. She couldn't believe the footwear most women her age wore out in public. It was no wonder married men were always after her.

She took Marty his burrito and a Budweiser. "The last supper, huh," he said, thumbing the hot foil, "before it's hotdogs and apple juice for two months."

April looked at him wearily through half eyes. "We'll see," she said.

"We're gonna get on fine," Marty said brightly. He lifted his burrito up with both hands, spilling some of the contents onto his lap. "Mouse is a good kid."

"How do you know what kind of kid she is? You haven't seen her in years."

"Lay off, would you? Sound like my ex." He made a talking puppet with his hand and spoke in his falsetto. "*Mah, mah, mah, mah, mah.*"

"What time does she get in?"

Marty picked a bean off his crotch and tossed it into his mouth. "Four-oh-eight. You gonna come along for the pickup?"

"You know I hate airports, Marty. *And* Traverse City. Can't stand the way those people drive."

Marty sighed and peered out the window. It was a quiet, purple dusk. "Anyway," he said, "I'm gonna go see if I can get any bites."

He went to the kitchen and returned with the last two beers still dangling from their plastic netting. He loosened one of them and gave it to April. In his other hand he held a little tin of black soil that was teeming with night crawlers. He had three or four of these tins, which he kept in the produce drawer of the refrigerator.

Monk Pond was a swampy, stinking thing that stretched a half mile or so across. Ownership was technically shared by the two or three dozen houses and trailers that surrounded it, but Marty was one of only two residents who actually had a boat and spent any time on the water. The other was an old nut named Forrest who walked around the pond once each day. If you were unlucky enough to be out in your yard when he passed, he'd invite himself on over and talk your ear off about the second amendment, or his part-time job at the antique mall. Forrest was personally into some weird stuff; old Barbie collectibles, torture devices from movie sets, real human baby parts in jars of formaldehyde.

Marty's little aqua-blue rowboat was littered with duct tape patches, and its scratched-up oars were different lengths. The boat's interior was splintery and stained with fish blood and who knew what else. April wouldn't set foot in the thing.

She stood at the window and watched him drag the boat from the backyard into the water by a thin gray rope, then he rowed out a short ways. He lit a cigarette and laid back in the boat, a single hand balancing the fishing pole across his chest. Marty claimed to have caught a forty-pound tiger muskie several years ago, up on Lake Superior. Said he took it to a taxidermist and everything, but then wasn't able to get it across the border, back into the states. Something about customs regulations. He'd returned it to the taxidermist for safekeeping, promised he'd be back for it. His passport had since expired, and he hadn't bothered to go retrieve the thing. April was skeptical about the whole story; no photographs, no witnesses.

The moon was like a see-through communion wafer against the dark blue sky. Dragonflies skirted through the reeds, and a turtle's head appeared at the water's surface, then quickly dipped beneath. Yellow lights twinkled across the pond. April watched Marty ease himself lower in the boat until all she could see of him was the gentle pulsing column of cigarette smoke against the black water.

The Mouse walked in through the kitchen screen door and it banged like a shot behind her. She was bigger than April had expected a ten-year-old would be. She was a smug-looking thing with dark, wild hair and one arched eyebrow. She looked nothing like Marty. April wondered if that was a sure thing.

April was sitting on the kitchen counter with a magazine across her lap. She stubbed out her cigarette.

"Hola," said the Mouse.

April slid off the counter. "Is that all you have?"

The Mouse was wearing a ratty pink backpack over one shoulder and she tapped a little silver pocketbook against her thigh.

"No, Marty's got my suitcase. My mom said I don't have to call him Dad unless I want to."

April shrugged. "Well, my name's April but you can call me whatever you want. So long as it's not a b-word or a c-word." The Mouse stared at her. "Anyway," April said, "you want me to call you Mouse like your dad does?"

"Whatever," the Mouse said. "Or Tracy. I don't care. I really do not care."

The Mouse stood on her tiptoes to investigate the wooden duck that rested on the fireplace mantel. She grabbed it by the bill, with her fist. "This is heavy," she said. The duck was missing one of its black marble eyeballs, and the Mouse dug a little bit at the remaining one with her fingertips.

April made sandwiches for the three of them. The Mouse wolfed down her peanut butter and jelly and asked why the milk tasted like water.

"It's skim," April said.

"Oh, I'm used to 2 percent."

"Next time," Marty said.

"Skim is better if you want to keep your figure," April said.

Marty was nervous, chewing fast and making bad jokes and asking the Mouse a lot of questions. He had a crack in the corner of his lip and it twinkled with fresh blood. The Mouse didn't like school, had never skied, and she didn't have a boyfriend, gross. She told them about the solar eclipse she and her classmates had watched out in the schoolyard several months earlier—she seemed to think that was a really big deal. She wanted to be on TV when she grew up.

"By the way, is your TV in color?" she asked.

Marty shook his head. "Why, is yours?"

"No," the Mouse said. "I just thought maybe you would have one. Shelly's got a color TV."

She got up from the table and opened the cupboard beneath the TV. She pulled out a stack of hunting magazines and a doorknob and a deck of playing cards with a silhouetted man in a cowboy hat on the box and the back of each card.

"Hey, Marty," she said. "Why was six afraid of seven?"

April had heard this one from some guy at a bar. "Because seven ate nine," she cut in.

The Mouse scowled at her.

Marty laughed. "You know any more?"

"Maybe," the Mouse said, with a measure of coolness. She pointed out the window. "Are them geese?"

Marty followed her finger and nodded. "They nested on the pond, been here all spring."

"Look at the babies," she said, pointing again. "One, two, three, four, five, six, seven. Can we feed 'em?" She gripped the windowsill with both hands and balanced on one foot with the other one propped up at the knee, like a flamingo. Her flip-flops were translucent purple.

Marty turned to April. "Have we got some store bread, hon?"

April said, "That's supposed to be for us, but sure, give them a piece or two."

She gave Marty the remaining half loaf of bread. The Mouse retrieved her rain boots from her suitcase and sashayed out to wade in the water.

April rinsed their plates and once Marty had left, she snuck a swig from the handle of whiskey she'd stowed under the sink, behind the cleaning supplies.

She watched an episode of *Flo* that she'd seen before. Marty and the Mouse were still chattering away out back when the show was over, and when April looked out the window, she saw that he was steadying the rowboat for the Mouse as she crawled in. They rowed out to the center of the pond. Marty had left the empty plastic bread bag on the lawn, and a mild wind dragged it slowly somersaulting across the backyard.

They called Marty's place a two-bedroom, but that was a stretch. Both bedrooms were tiny, one seven-by-seven and the other eight-by-eight, and both bordered the living room, which opened to the kitchen. All the walls were paper thin. The burnt-orange carpeting was worn down bald and didn't absorb any noise, nor did any of the threadbare upholstery.

The Mouse talked loudly in her sleep, and she was up at 7:00 a.m. on the nose every morning, stirring around in the bathroom then clattering through the refrigerator. Sometimes she went outdoors first thing in the morning to putter around the lawn and into the pond in her boots, to feed the geese if they were nearby. She never eased the screen door shut behind her; no matter what time of day, she let it swing free to crash violently behind her.

April didn't trust the Mouse. She was sneaky. She ate too much. They went through a box of Apple Jacks in three days. She always had that one-eyed "is-that-so?" look on her face, and she was seldom fully clothed. She scampered around in shorts and a yellow bikini top with triangles the size of sugar packets over her flat chest.

Marty, on the other hand, was really getting into this parenting thing. He was still on disability, so he had all the time in the world for the Mouse. He took her to the park and to lunch at Arby's and for cherry-lime rickeys at the ice cream place. He took her all the way to The Cherry Hut, a forty-five minute drive each way, just for one piece of pie. He taught her some silly song about a little man who lived on a red moon, and they sang that song day in and day out. The Mouse was completely tone-deaf, which April pointed out to Marty one time and he said, "Your point being?"

He took the Mouse out fishing in the evening while April drank whiskeys and changed the color of her nails.

When the Mouse caught her first fish, Marty made April get the camera to take a picture of the little thing while it was still alive, wiggling and glittering on the hook. The Mouse didn't even flinch when Marty beheaded and filleted it on the back porch. April thought that was a little sick.

Later that night, April went to The Blue Slipper and stayed there until last call. Men bought her drinks all night long; she didn't spend a dime. Marty didn't even notice that April was out past 2:00 a.m. He was fast asleep when she crawled into bed, snoring like a hog and unresponsive when she started rubbing up on him. April half-wished there had been some new men in town, someone else she could start up with if Marty wasn't going to give a hoot. Marty was the nicest guy she'd ever been with by a long shot, and they'd been together for almost three years now, but it's not like she didn't have other options. Men were always trying to start up with her. Unfortunately at The Blue Slipper, it was just the same-old same-olds.

The next afternoon, April applied tanning oil and Marty drove the three of them out to Lake Michigan. There were only a few others on the beach, a couple dozen people perhaps, if that, and April wished she had more of an audience for her new bikini.

The Mouse was positively giddy on this beach, like she'd never set foot on sand before, never seen a gull or held a shell in her hand. April watched as the two of them pounced into waves. When they returned, they were deep in conversation, and April overheard enough to discover that the Mouse didn't know how to swim. Not very well, anyway. She could keep her head above water, but had never been properly trained and couldn't stay up for any amount of time, or go any amount of distance. Already, she had spent lots of time in Monk Pond, but now that April thought about it, she realized she'd never seen the Mouse go out past waist deep.

Marty was saying, "Don't worry, Mouse. I'll give you lessons back in the pond. It's too choppy out here to get a good session in. I had no idea you didn't know how to swim, woulda thought someone had taught you by now."

April said, "Crazy that you don't know how to swim for as much time as you spend in the water. Guess you must be a starfish, huh?"

The Mouse looked up at her. "Why a starfish?"

"They're the only fish that can't swim," April explained.

Marty gave April an unpleasant look and quickly interjected. "*But*," he said, lifting a wise finger to the Mouse, "starfish are special. When they lose one of their legs, they up and grow it right back."

The Mouse seemed satisfied with this information.

April formulated a snide joke about a new leg just being more dead weight, being as the thing still couldn't swim, but she didn't share this aloud.

The following morning, the Mouse burst into their bedroom with a fistful of stale bread.

"One of 'em disappeared!" she cried. She was panting. She set down the bread and dropped her hands to her knees to catch her breath. Marty threw the blanket over April even though she was wearing a T-shirt.

"It's true," the Mouse said. She was in her rain boots and navy mesh shorts and a yellow bikini top. She was wearing one of Marty's baseball caps with the plastic snap panel in the back adjusted to fit her, but the bill stretched beyond her little head in both directions and it was so low on her brow that she had to tilt her head back to see out from under it. "I was feeding 'em, then all the sudden, there's a little *shwoop* and this little goose gets sucked under the water, and just like that," the Mouse snapped her fingers, "it just disappears."

She paused for a moment, allowing them time to react, then continued, "So then the other little geese looked at it, where it had been, and there's just some ripples in the water—"

"Mouse," Marty propped himself on his elbow to face her. "Relax. I think it was your imagination. It was probably just lagging."

"No," she insisted. "I always count 'em when they come over. And there was seven when they came, seven babies and the mama. Then I counted 'em again and again to make sure, and I swear there's only six."

The Mouse stared hard at April for a moment and said, "You look really different in the morning." She turned back to Marty. "What should we do?"

"You steer clear of the pond, Mouse," he said. "I'll check it out later."

That evening, when the geese returned for their routine nightly feeding, sure enough, Marty reported to April, there were only six goslings.

"Strangest thing," he said.

The Mouse, vindicated, nodded emphatically at Marty's side. Her eyes shone bright and exultant under the porch light, which was swarming with moths and mosquitoes and mayflies. Marty spat on the ground in a tight, practiced stream.

"Yeah," April said dramatically. "*So* strange. I can't even imagine."

The Mouse swatted at a mayfly and said, "These things have a life expectancy of one day. Do you know how many eggs they lay in one day?"

"Ten," April said.

"Eight thousand," said the Mouse. "My dad told me that."

The Mouse had a bad dream that night about a pond monster, and Marty had to go hold her to calm her down. When he came back to bed, April tickled up his thigh with her fingers. He edged away from her.

"So are we just not gonna do it until August? I got needs, Marty."

"We can do it quiet," he said, patting her hand, "Just not tonight, I'm tuckered."

April got up and poured herself a coffee cup full of whiskey and watched the TV on mute until the Mouse came out of her bedroom. Her hair was matted flat against one side of her head and her face was pink, her eyes shrunken with sleep, nightgown bunched in her fists. She pointed at the TV and said, "That flashing light's bugging me under the door." April was too drunk to argue and she wasn't really following the program she was watching anyway, so she turned the TV off and went to bed.

The very next morning, the Mouse came charging into their bedroom again.

"Geez," Marty grunted. "We knock here, compadre, remember?"

"*I saw it*," she said, breathless and clutching her chest.

"Saw what?"

"The monster," the Mouse whispered in utter terror, as though it might overhear. "*This long*." She stretched her arms out as wide as she could in both directions. "Its head is like this." She made a coconut-sized ball with her hands. "And teeth." She bared and snapped her own teeth. "It was slithering around like a snake in our yard, then it disappeared into the water."

"*Right*," April said. "A pond monster in our own backyard." She had a roaring headache and she was so nauseous that their hard, flat mattress felt like a quivering waterbed beneath her.

Marty said, "I don't think so, Mouse. I'm out there every day. No monsters."

The Mouse stomped one of her boots. It was still soaking wet and a thin kelly-green weed was spread across the toe. Her knees were starting to grow a little hair on them, and the fuzz shimmered like threads of white gold in the early-morning sun that streamed through the doorway.

"I saw it," the Mouse said again. "It ate that baby goose and now it's back for more."

"*Right-o*," April whispered mildly.

"It was the second-most scared I've ever been in my life," she said, gripping her bottom lip with her top teeth. "After the time my cousin Tom locked me in the refrigerator. I got butter on my head." Her teeth were coming in uneven, fangs first, and looked way too big for her head. She'd probably get the braces that Marty should've had, April thought. She wondered if the Mouse was going to cry. April really did not care, one way or the other. The room was hot as blazes and she was certain Marty would smell the whiskey on her. But he wasn't paying attention to her—he was staring at the Mouse.

He sat up and reached for his shirt, which was in a ball beside the bed. April groaned. She wiped her sweaty upper lip with the sheet and turned the other way. "Better go catch that monster, Marty," she said over her shoulder. "Holler if you need backup."

April slept all day, which was a good thing, because the Mouse was up all that night again, certain she heard movement in the grass outside her window. Marty was in and out of bed so many times to console the Mouse that April lost track. He finally dragged the Mouse's pillow and blanket into their bedroom and set her up on the floor next to his side of the bed. April heard him kiss her forehead.

"Nighty-night," he whispered.

"You're babying her," April said the next morning.

Marty said, "I just want her to feel safe here."

"Kids need to work that stuff out on their own. I grew up without a dad altogether, and I turned out just fine, didn't I? You can't make up for ten years in one summer. You should quit trying so hard."

"April, you're bein' a bit of a bitch."

April yawned into her shoulder.

The geese weren't there the next morning, and they didn't show up that evening, or the next day either. The Mouse was gutted. She stood in the backyard for long stretches, clutching a piece of bread with one hand and using the other to cup around her mouth while she yelled encouraging messages across the pond and into the sky. There was no sign of them. And the Mouse's nightmares didn't improve either; she started migrating to the floor of their bedroom every single night, and once she even crawled up into their bed.

"Oh, for crying out loud," April whispered when she woke to shuffling on the far edge of bed and realized what was going on.

"What?" the Mouse said in a challenging tone. "I'm *scared*."

April stared at the Mouse. "Do you have friends at school?" she said.

"Tons."

Marty said, "Let's all try and get some sleep."

"You two have your slumber party," April said. She went to the living room and smoked three cigarettes with the windows closed then fell asleep on the couch.

Marty had to help a buddy out with a busted sump pump the next afternoon and he asked April to keep an eye on the Mouse. April protested, told him that her day was pretty much packed, but he assured her that the Mouse would entertain herself. April was cleaning the kitchen while the Mouse played outside, when she heard Forrest's voice through the screen door, asking the Mouse what was new. She heard the Mouse giving Forrest her full account of the pond monster; the disappearance of the gosling, the recent sighting.

"Whattya reckon it is, Forrest?" the Mouse said.

Forrest said, "Kid, there's a lot about this world that we're never gonna know, and we're probably all better off that way."

April laid down on the couch to take a nap.

The Mouse returned a while later with a chestful of mail, all for Marty. The Mouse eagerly collected the mail every day; she seemed to be expecting a letter that never arrived. She sat with April and they watched TV in silence for an hour or so. A commercial for Gatorade came on, featuring several athletes including the Buffalo Bills' quarterback.

The Mouse brightened and said, "My granddad played for the Bills."

"Is that right?" April figured if this was true, she'd have surely heard about it from Marty by now, although he didn't ever have much to say about Tracy's mom.

"Yep," said the Mouse. "My mom's dad. He was a star. He's gonna take me and my mom to a game this fall," she continued. "He told us he could get us some sideline seats."

"Is that right?" said April.

The Mouse got some leftovers out of the refrigerator and brought them into the living room. She ate chicken wings from a damp, lidded cardboard box. When she finished, she tossed the box full of bones onto the floor and wiped her dirty fingers into the couch. April was deeply annoyed. She wanted the Mouse to take that trash back into the kitchen. She wanted her to wash her hands and also to clean the orange off her face, to realize that it was there without April having to point it out.

During the next commercial break, the Mouse asked April how old she was.

April said, "Forty."

The Mouse said, "That is *so* old. That is so old, I don't think I'll even live that long."

April scowled at her and said, "What're you gonna do, jump off a bridge the day before your fortieth birthday?" As she spoke these words, she considered that they might not be appropriate conversation for a ten-year-old, but then again, the ten-year-old had started it.

The Mouse laughed. April laughed.

Then April asked the Mouse if she wanted to paint nails.

"Mm." The Mouse made a face. "Nah."

"How come?" April said. "You spend so much time rooting around, I bet you could really use a manicure."

"No thanks." The Mouse got up from the couch. "OK, I'm gonna go play outside."

April felt like she'd been insulted. "Come on," she said. "I used to do it for a job before I met your dad. I'm real good at it and I've got tons of colors."

The Mouse bit her lip and slowly drew her hands behind her back.

"What are you doing?" April rose to her feet.

"Nothing." The Mouse backed toward the door.

April followed her with sudden adrenaline. "What are you *doing*?"

The Mouse turned to bolt outside, and April grabbed her arm. "What have you got?"

The Mouse squealed and twisted away from April. April looked down at the Mouse's wrist, which she had in a tight grip. The Mouse had her hand balled in a small fist, but April caught a glimpse of her fingertips. The Mouse's fingernails were sloppily painted a deep red, flecks of stray polish lining the flesh surrounding her nails.

"Where'd you get *that*?" April said. "Huh, you little thief? Where'd you get *my shade*?"

The Mouse shrieked, "Let go of me!"

Marty was bounding in through the kitchen screen door. "The hell is going on?" he shouted.

April dropped the Mouse's arm. "She's just squawking 'cause she got caught. She's wearing my shade, Marty." April pointed at the Mouse's hands. "Which means she went through my stuff. My basket, which is in the closet, which she knows is *off limits*."

The Mouse was rubbing her arm. She was flushed and her nostrils were flared. She wasn't crying.

Marty looked helplessly at the Mouse. "Trace," he said, "You knew the score. Did you go through April's stuff?"

"Nope," the Mouse said.

Marty looked back at April.

April threw her hands in the air. "Why don't you ask her to show you her polish, ask her where she got that shade? Geez Almighty, Marty." April turned to the Mouse. "Did you really think I wouldn't notice, you little thief? Or you thought I'd fall for your lies like your daddy here does?"

The Mouse snorted. "I used your dumb shade, OK? OK? And no, I *didn't* think you'd notice. You don't pay no attention to me. I was bored so I went into your room and used your dumb shade. But I'm not a liar." She rammed her chin out. "You know what? You're trash, just like my mom said."

April lunged at the Mouse, but Marty blocked her. The Mouse cowered behind him, wearing a triumphant face. "Outside, *now*," he bellowed over his shoulder at the Mouse, and she went.

Marty gripped April's biceps firmly with his thumbs and she struggled against him.

"You're gonna let her talk to me like that?"

"No, babe, but you need to settle. She's just a kid. Geez Almighty."

April was in her highest heels, which put her at exactly eye level with Marty. She was trembling with indignation, radiantly angry. "It's me or the Mouse, Marty. Your choice."

"Shush now."

"I won't have a little liar insulting me like that in my house."

"She's only here for a few more weeks is all, anyhow." Marty stroked her arms shoulder to wrist without loosening his grasp.

April wiggled free and stepped back from him. She sniffed and shrugged coolly. "If she's not on a bus back to Buffalo tomorrow, I'm outta here, Marty, and I ain't comin' back."

"Geez Almighty." Marty wiped his fingers over his mouth.

"She's a liar and a sneak, Marty, I can't believe you won't see through it. She's trying to get between us. She weaseled her way into our bedroom with this *monster* business, then she snoops through my stuff, lies about it . . ."

Marty took his camouflage hat off and put it right back on. His chest was brown and deflated underneath his white V-neck T-shirt. He glanced over April's head, out the window.

April grabbed his chin and squared it to her own. "How long I been with you, Marty? How good am I to you? And you're gonna let someone stay under our roof that talks to me that way? She comes in all cozying up to you, all wanting to be family with you, but nothing's been the same with *us* since she came. *I'm* your family, Marty."

Marty breathed loud and long through his nose. "It's a few more weeks is all," he said. "You know? I haven't even taught her how to swim yet."

"A few more weeks, *then* what?" April scoffed. "You don't see her for another five years? Or maybe she stays with us for a few weeks next summer, eats us out of house and home again, and disrespects me like she does, then what? Then what, the same thing the next summer?"

Marty's face was so tired and hollow.

April sighed and ran the back of her middle finger over his cheek. She made her voice sweeter. "Marty, you tried. We tried. It ain't gonna work. We ain't cut out for this."

Marty drove the toe of his tennis shoe hard into the carpet, but he didn't argue. He closed his eyes and massaged his eye sockets with the heel of his hands. He went to the bathroom and blew his nose into a piece of toilet paper, then went outside to find the Mouse.

That night, April slept at her friend Linda's house, and the Mouse was gone by the time she came home the next afternoon. The little bedroom was entirely empty. The twin bed was stripped, the lamp with the torn purple shade returned to the living room, the comforter stuffed back into the closet.

April used a falling-apart cardboard box to move her things from the master bedroom back to the little one. She balanced the box on her knee while she loaded it up, and made it into the small room just before the bottom seam gave. She happily unloaded her things into the dresser. It was empty except for a single barrette in the back corner of the bottom drawer.

She ate yogurt from a cup, then poured herself a whiskey.

She decided to try and get Marty cheered up with some company that evening. She didn't like to see him this way, all mopey and listless. This was for the best, she had to remind herself, and he'd snap out of it before too long. A whiskey or two and he'd remember how good life was before the Mouse ever showed up.

April invited Randall and Denise from across the pond over for dinner. Randall and Denise didn't have kids either, and they were always a good time. April had prepared a tater tot casserole and bought an angel food cake, along with a carton of Cool Whip and a jar of strawberry syrup. It was Marty's favorite. She served whiskey sodas in sixteen-ounce Detroit Lions game cups. Denise had brought a six-pack of wine coolers for herself.

She offered one to April, but April could see that she wasn't too eager to share.

"Love your outfit, April," Denise said.

"You've seen all this before."

Midway through the meal, Randall leaned away from the table onto the back two legs of his chair, hooking his knees beneath the table's edge to balance. He wiped his napkin over his black goatee and said, "So did y'all hear about that snakehead?"

"Not at the dinner table, Randall," Denise said. She turned to April. "This is gross."

"Snakehead fish," Randall continued. "Right out here." He jerked his thumb over his shoulder, in the direction of the pond. "God-awful things, from Asia, I reckon."

"What is it now?" April said.

"*Nasty* suckers," Randall said. "They get three, four feet long and they've got these big teeth. Meat eaters. Go after other fish, frogs, birds, each other, whatever they can find."

April swallowed hard. The hot casserole in her mouth went down slow and tight in her throat. She looked at Denise, who shuddered to confirm the story. Marty had stopped eating. Denise finished her wine cooler and handed Randall another one from the six-pack at her feet. Randall came crashing forward onto the front legs of his chair and rose to access his back pocket. He pulled out a single loose key and popped the top off her cooler after a few tries.

"Worst part about these snakeheads," Randall continued, sitting back down, "is they come up outta the water. They can survive on land for days. Move like this." He swiveled his arm back and forth in a tight slither.

"Randall, *please*," Denise said, absently peeling the label off her cooler. "We're eating."

"What on earth are they doing in our pond?" April said quietly.

"Who knows," Randall said. "I wonder if some jackass didn't bring one in to get rid of the geese or something, keep 'em from shittin' all over our lawns. You notice how all them geese disappeared?"

"Mm," April said.

"Well, who knows. But Jake, you know Jake? He caught one of these snakeheads the other night, and he reckons he's seen at least two or three more."

April said, "I'll believe it when I see it."

She glanced sideways at Marty.

He was staring out at the pond.

April cleared her throat and tipped her cup toward her in order to draw a small black bug out the side of her whiskey with her fingertip. She smeared the bug into her thigh.

"Who wants seconds of something?" she said.

"Hey, Marty," Randall said, "That's really somethin', isn't it, a snakehead fish in our pond. Isn't that somethin' else?"

"Yeah," Marty said softly, still peering out the window.

He wore an expression April had not seen on him before. Something else escaped his lips and April didn't ask him to repeat it.

She followed his gaze out the window. A few scarlet streaks of daylight remained at the horizon. Cattails shuffled like sleepy dancers in the breeze. A skin of mint-green algae covered the outer edge of the pond, and beyond it the water looked as thick and black as ink.

REAL

GOLD

Laura and Shelly were in the same Sunday School class, even though in real school they were two grades apart. They got along fine at church but Shelly didn't really speak to her at real school, so Laura was surprised to receive an invite to Shelly's birthday party sleepover in her parents' church mailbox one Sunday. She hoped it was Shelly's idea, not her mother's. The invite had a navy rubber-stamped cupcake on the back seam of the envelope and a small yellow crumb smashed flat onto it. Laura's mother called Shelly's mother to RSVP Laura's "yes" to the birthday party. Laura picked out a lip gloss set for Shelly at Target. She wrapped it in tissue paper and put it in a flashy birthday bag with headphones and roller skates all over the outside.

• • •

There were nine girls at the sleepover. Laura was the youngest and the smallest, and the only one with short hair. She'd recently gotten it cut up to her chin after her favorite girl on television had hers cut that way, but it didn't sit the same on Laura, whose hair just went high and wild at this length. For the party, she wore half of it pulled up on the top of her head with a little green band. She was hoping it would grow out a lot before school in the fall. Laura was also the only girl there without a proper sleeping bag. Her family didn't camp, so her mother had sent her with a comforter in a zippered transparent plastic case and said if Laura folded it over twice it would be just like a sleeping bag.

Shelly's house smelled like Shelly's clothing always smelled at church and her basement had big squares of wiry blue carpeting laid across the cement floor, a television, and a few beanbag chairs. Beneath the staircase sat a washer-dryer, a few big bags of cat food, a wicker basket of potatoes, a cardboard box full of books crumbling at the spines. The girls laid out their sleeping bags on the carpeted floor of the basement, five of them lined up next to one another across the center of the room and the others perpendicular, at their heads and at their feet. Laura introduced herself to the girls she would be sleeping next to.

Kimberly, on Laura's left, was friends with Shelly from horse-riding camp, where they were in the same cabin even though they rode different styles. Shelly rode English, Kimberly explained, whereas she rode Western. Kimberly's horse at camp was a big gray stud horse named Zipper.

Laura had never ridden a horse. "Were you scared the first time?" she asked.

"No," said Kimberly. "You just get on and the horse pretty much knows what to do. Zipper bucked once, but I didn't even fall."

The girl on Laura's right was a head taller than all the other girls there, and one of her eyebrows was more arched than the other, which gave her a mean look. She had very pretty, blackish eyes. A thick dry-looking line of dark lipstick circled the outside of her lips. She said she was Shelly's cousin, and Shelly's next-door neighbor too. Her name was Tracy. She was thirteen years old. Laura asked if she had Shelly's last name.

"No," Tracy said, "Because it's our moms that are sisters. They don't speak anymore, our moms, but they still let Shelly and me be friends."

"Are your moms in a fight?" Laura asked.

"Yeah," Tracy said. "I think it's something about my dad." She had silver wraparound sunglasses pushed back over her forehead and she adjusted them. "He's pretty much outta the picture, my dad, but I think it's something about him. My dad's like a professional fisherman," she continued.

"Yeah?"

"He caught a forty-pound tiger muskie in Lake Superior."

"Geez oh Pete!" Laura said. She hadn't a clue what this meant.

Tracy continued to discuss her life. She had a boyfriend from Cheektowaga. He lived right next to the Buffalo International Airport and could hear jets coming and going all night long, she said. Sometimes when he and Tracy were on the phone and a big one came, he would hold his phone out the window so she could hear it too. They were pretty serious for their age, she said. Her boyfriend was fifteen and part Indian. She showed Laura a faraway picture of a guy in a football helmet.

"My granddad played for the Bills," Tracy said. "So anyway, I'm real into football players."

Laura complimented Tracy's boyfriend, then Tracy's gold bracelet.

Tracy spun the bracelet over her wrist bone. "It's real gold," she said. "So how do you know Shelly?"

"We go to the same church."

Tracy wore a T-shirt knotted at one side so her whole stomach showed. She tightened the knot. "Oh, eff church," she said.

Laura felt her jaw fall open. She felt like she might want to say that too.

For dinner, Shelly's mother served sloppy-joe sandwiches and macaroni and cheese from a glass casserole pan. The girls sat on the floor with paper plates. "You can give your scraps to my cat," Shelly said. She went to the screen door and scooted a cinder block over to prop it open. A little black cat trotted in the door. It had a crust in one of its eyes. It licked sloppy-joe juice from Laura's plate. Shelly got out a long piece of white elastic with a catnip-filled sack tied around one end. The cat leapt wildly after the toy when Shelly drew it across the floor and made it fly through the air.

Tracy said, "That stupid cat scratched my dog's nose up."

"That's because your stupid dog was snapping at her," Shelly said.

The girls talked about pets and gym class and television. Kimberly told a story about the pet iguana in her homeroom, how some kid let it crawl up his shoulder and through his hair until it bit his ear. Laura tried to add a few small things to the conversation at sensible times, hoping Shelly would notice how well she was fitting in with the older group, but everything she said got lost or covered up by louder voices. When the girls got onto summer vacations, the places they had gone and all the places they dreamt of visiting, Laura wanted to tell them about the Zen gardens in Japan that she had just learned about in Geography class. They were called the Ryōan-ji gardens, and the picture in her textbook was so beautiful that she had torn it out to keep for herself. Her Geography book was really beat-up anyway; she was certain no one would notice. The photograph showed a glassy black pool filled with orange fish, and a little gray-haired gardener in a kimono. But by the time she thought to offer this to the list of destinations, the other girls were already on to another topic. They talked about their boyfriends. Laura didn't have a boyfriend yet, none of her friends her age did, but she was starting to think she might be ready by the time school started this fall, depending how much the boys in her class had matured over the summer. Or better yet, she thought, if she and Shelly got to be friends at real school, maybe one of the older boys in Shelly's class would want to be Laura's boyfriend.

The birthday cake was marble with Funfetti icing, and Shelly's trick candles sparked and relit even after she'd blown them out. She got a second wish, and a third, before all the candles were completely dead.

She said, "It's my birthday so we used paper plates instead of the regular ones, so I don't have to load the dishwasher. I have to do it every night usually."

One of the other girls piped up and said, "I have to do that too, then unload it when I get home from school."

Laura thought hers was just as good as anybody's, so she said, "I have to vacuum cleaner the whole house every Saturday." The other girls actually heard her this time, and she found herself suddenly unnerved by the attention of everyone in the room. She couldn't tell how it was going over. Her voice sounded tiny and peculiar to her own ears.

Tracy said, "I have to do that too. But you should do what I do, if your mom doesn't pay too close attention: just run the vacuum over the floor so it makes the stripes, but you don't actually have to sweep."

"That's a really good idea," Laura agreed, and some of the other girls said they were going to start doing that too.

Tracy asked Shelly if she could have a Tylenol. "I'm on my period," she explained to the group. "Are any of you having periods yet? Probably not."

When Shelly disappeared to the bathroom to retrieve a Tylenol, Kimberly asked the girls if any of them had played Light as a Feather. "We could do it after dark," she said. "Light as a feather, stiff as a board. It's really scary."

"No it's not," Tracy said. "It's not real. I did it once and we dropped my friend Ashley."

Kimberly looked down into the carpet. She picked at a single thread, pulling and twisting it until it was scraggly and longer than the others.

Tracy said, "I'll tell you what's scary, though, is Bloody Mary. Anybody done that?"

None of the girls had played Bloody Mary.

Tracy picked up her Styrofoam cup and shook the ice. "We'll play later," she said. "But don't say anything about it in front of Linda," she nodded down the hallway, in the direction of Shelly's mother. "She does church and she's really uptight."

She turned suddenly to Laura. "You do church too."

"Just because I have to," Laura said, her face immediately hot like she'd been caught in a lie.

Shelly returned a few minutes later and someone asked her what birthday presents she'd gotten from her mother.

"A jean jacket," Shelly said, "and a pair of riding pants and a Baby-Sitter's Club book set. And now my allowance will be a dollar more. I'm saving for a camera."

One of the other girls said, "I'm saving for a phone and it's going to take forever."

"You guys should do this," Tracy said, "if you want more allowance. My dad, he lives in Michigan but he sends me an allowance every week, and I says to my dad a while back, because we're talking about making my allowance more, and I says, because I just learned this in school, 'How about if we make my allowance one penny a week, and double it every week?'"

The girls thought about this for a little bit.

Tracy said, "My dad even agreed to it and I'm up to two dollars something." She laughed. "He hasn't figured it out yet, he's so funny."

"Hasn't figured what out yet?" somebody asked.

"This," Tracy said, "I'll show you."

Tracy went to a kitchen drawer and returned with a piece of Best Western stationary and a short, yellow eraser-less pencil. The girls crowded around Tracy while she wrote out a series of additions and multiplications to demonstrate how quickly the amount got huge. She was going to start getting a whole lot of money from her dad soon.

"See?" Tracy said.

All of the girls were impressed, except for Shelly, who seemed very annoyed. She stood at the window with her cat in her arms. It bit her spaghetti strap over and over again.

Kimberly said, "I'm telling that to my mother tomorrow."

Laura stared at the paper. She wanted Tracy to keep going and going, to see the numbers go higher and higher and higher, to infinity.

Shelly's mother hooked up the karaoke machine in the living room. The microphone crackled, and when Kimberly sang, she danced so hard that she accidentally pulled the cord right out of its socket. When Shelly sang, her mother said, "You have such a nice singing voice." All of the girls took a turn except for Tracy.

When it was time to do presents, Laura went to the basement to retrieve her bag for Shelly. She sifted through her backpack, setting aside her toothbrush with a square of toilet paper wrapped around the brush, travel toothpaste, a half bar of soap and navy washcloth.

She remembered as she looked over her nighttime things that while packing that afternoon, she had chosen to leave Marshall at home. She now pictured the small stuffed terrycloth walrus slouched on her nightstand in her dark bedroom. It was the first sleepover she hadn't brought him to; it would be the first night she hadn't slept with Marshall since getting him five or six years ago at SeaWorld.

Laura pulled out Shelly's gift bag and fiddled with one of the corners that had been crumpled beneath her other things. It was the right decision not to bring Marshall—none of the other girls had brought overnight animals, that she'd seen. A girl who was nearly ready for a boyfriend shouldn't be sleeping with a stuffed animal anyway. She was old enough to know that Marshall was just a toy without feelings. He didn't need her at night. And, as she thought about it more, she realized that she didn't need Marshall any more than he needed her. It was the right decision, and she didn't even miss him. With this knowledge Laura felt very grown-up and a little bit guilty, as though she ought to apologize to Marshall and to her own childhood self for abandoning them both so easily.

The girls went outside after presents so Shelly's mom could take their picture together on the back porch. A soupy dusk settled in like warm breath. A dog approached the porch and Shelly's mother grabbed its collar to keep it out of the picture until she was finished. The dog was handsome and gray, wolflike with light eyes and small pupils. After the pictures were done, Tracy went to the dog and she knelt down and curled his ears around in her fingers. She reached for the faded tennis ball from its teeth.

"Give it, Caesar," she said.

The dog released the ball, leapt a few feet back from her and bounced on its hind legs, gasping in anticipation. Tracy threw the ball and Caesar dashed after it. Tracy wiped the palm of her hands on her shorts.

"Did you guys see that scar on Caesar's nose?" she said. "It's from Shelly's cat. It bled real bad. I hate cats."

"Me too," said Kimberly, "Dogs are so much better."

Several other girls agreed, right in front of Shelly, but not Laura. She thought Shelly might appreciate that, if she noticed.

The bathroom in the basement was unfinished, with floor tiles scattered across the base of the shower, the hot faucet handle missing, exposing a single gleaming pencil-sized post, and the top lid of the toilet propped on its side against the counter, its rust-colored underbelly facing out.

The girls crowded into the bathroom. Tracy lit a thick candle in a jar that smelled like cinnamon and set it on the counter, then she turned off the light. There was a thin line of yellow at the base of the door, so Tracy grabbed a towel from the shower rod and shoved it into the crack so that the candle provided the only light in the room.

"Bloody Mary," Tracy said, addressing the girls by way of the mirror, "was the Queen of England. She killed a bunch of people, ordered them to be burnt at the stake and had a bunch of babies stabbed onto the end of spears and hoisted up for everybody to look at while they rotted and smelled."

A few of the girls giggled.

Tracy continued, "They say Bloody Mary's ghost can be summoned by saying her name thirteen times in a dark room in front of a mirror. That if you do that with a group, all chanting her name together with your eyes closed then open your eyes together, her face will be in the mirror."

Kimberly said, "Holy cow."

"Yeah," nodded Tracy. "I know."

"This seems sort of bad, though," Shelly said. She was looking sideways at the girls next to her rather than in the mirror. "I didn't know this was gonna be so bad. Did you guys?"

"Bad?" Tracy scoffed. "*Bad.* What do you mean, *bad*?"

Laura knew what Shelly meant by bad, but she didn't say anything.

"Remember," Tracy continued, ignoring Shelly and eyeing them all in the reflection of the mirror. "We say Bloody Mary thirteen times. Count in your head. OK? Eyes closed now, and nobody peeks until we get to thirteen otherwise she won't be summoned."

Laura looked at Shelly last before closing her eyes. Shelly looked miserable. Laura wondered if she was going to peek.

"Bloody Mary," Tracy spoke in a raspy, ominous whisper.

"Bloody Mary, Bloody Mary," the others joined and the chant grew.

Laura felt cold and jumpy. She wanted to open her eyes.

"Bloody Mary," the girls murmured, "Bloody Mary." Their voices collected into one pitch and one rhythm. The pace quickened, led by Tracy, whose voice was thicker and lower than the others.

"Bloody Mary, Bloody Mary," Laura made sure she was speaking loudly enough to be heard, so they would know she was doing it too, that just because she was younger and did church, that didn't mean she was more scared.

After the thirteenth Bloody Mary, Laura opened her eyes, her heart rattling in her ears with a pure and intense adrenaline. The reflection in the mirror snapped and trembled into place in front of her. She met the eyes of the other girls, all of them darting back and forth, some more scared than others, some quick to laugh with relief.

Tracy, a head above everyone else, glared into the mirror at the reflection. "Who peeked?" she said.

The girls were silent. Tracy picked up the candle and held it at her chin so her face was illuminated red. Her eyes rested on her own reflection in the mirror for just a moment and Laura watched as Tracy self-consciously adjusted her expression to be model-like, her chin up, eyes wider, lips pursed.

"I know somebody peeked," Tracy said, her gaze returning to the other girls. "Who peeked?"

She extended her arm so the candle was inches from the mirror and she swayed it back and forth fast enough that the flame flickered and followed the wick in a sleek golden trail, but it didn't go out.

No one spoke.

Tracy scowled. "Then we'll do it again."

Shelly was standing next to the door and she flicked the light on. The immediate brightness made big colored splotches behind Laura's eyes when she blinked.

Tracy barked, "What the hell?"

"I'm done," Shelly said. She snatched the candle from Tracy's hands and blew it out. The smoke rose in a single twisty white swirl.

"See," Tracy said nastily, "I knew it was you."

"I didn't peek," Shelly said. She licked her thumb and index finger and pinched the wick of the candle. It hissed and stopped smoking. "But I think this game is bad, and it's my birthday and I don't want to play anymore."

"Shelly, don't be such a lesbian," Tracy said.

Kimberly said, "Yeah, don't be a lesbian, Shelly."

Shelly looked like she had just been slapped.

"I'm just kidding, of course," Tracy said. "But if you guys are too scared to do this, I'm just going to have a smoke."

She pushed by Shelly, stepped over the towel on the ground, and walked out of the bathroom, her flip-flops clapping noisily against the cement floor.

"I was kidding too, Shelly," Kimberly said. "I know you're not a lesbian."

"I know," Shelly said.

The girls filed uncomfortably out of the bathroom.

There was a little glass dish of cinnamon hearts sitting on the lid of the washer, next to the box of powdered detergent. Shelly picked up one heart and sucked on it noisily. She passed the dish to Laura, who did the same thing. It was so spicy it made Laura's eyes water. When Shelly wasn't looking, she spat the heart into her palm where it made a bright red smear. Kimberly plucked a cinnamon heart out of the dish and crunched it down like it was a Skittle. She nodded toward the stairs where Tracy had just disappeared and said, "I want to watch her smoke. Can we watch from the kitchen?"

"It's not that cool," Shelly said. "She goes into her yard and it's just, well, let's just play karaoke again or something."

"No, let's watch," the freckled girl said.

Laura really wanted to watch too, but she kept quiet so she wouldn't upset Shelly.

The other girls didn't wait for Shelly's permission. Laura lagged behind with Shelly to show she was on her team, and at the top of the stairs, Shelly turned to her and said, "Don't tell your mom about Bloody Mary, OK? Or she might not let you come over again."

Upstairs, the other girls were gathered around the kitchen sink and peering out the window.

"Look," Kimberly whispered, pointing into the lawn beyond Shelly's backyard. You could see precisely where Shelly's backyard ended and Tracy's began, where the grass went from short and green and tidy to dry and weedy, littered with dog piles and a few aluminum cans.

Tracy stood next to a white plastic deck chair. She smoked with long, cool, lazy movements and smooth breaths, like she'd been doing it her whole life. She ashed her cigarette against the top of the chair. Caesar was at her thigh. She absently rolled her foot over a Nerf soccer ball.

On the other side of the kitchen, Shelly was rooting around noisily in the refrigerator and she said, "Does anyone want some Pepsi?"

"Doesn't her mom see?" one of the girls asked.

"Yeah," said another girl. "Shelly, doesn't her mom see?"

"No," Shelly said, sounding miffed, "because her mom works the night shift so she's always away. And when she is home she takes these pills that make her sleep all the time so she doesn't even notice when Tracy watches bad television, or when she smokes or her boyfriend comes over. She does whatever she wants."

Kimberly said, "That's so cool."

Shelly sniffed. "I guess, except that there are other things like she always has to do her own laundry and meals. Her house is a dump. She doesn't even have a bicycle. So it's not that cool, she's not really that cool so much as she acts like she is."

A few of the girls turned to look at Shelly, who sipped her soda from a straw and continued, "In fact, I don't know why she told that story about the penny and the big numbers. The money from her dad, the allowance. That doesn't happen. Her dad doesn't send her anything. He's out of the picture."

Kimberly said, "He doesn't send her money every week like she said?"

"No," said Shelly. She gazed triumphantly at the group. She had their attention now and her expression was serious but animated, like she was both burdened and pleased to be delivering such important news. "I don't know why she even told that story, because her dad's never sent her anything, not even for Christmas. Even *my dad* sends me stuff for Christmas."

"Not even for Christmas?" Kimberly said.

"No," said Shelly. "In fact . . ." She clapped her hand over her mouth. "I shouldn't. But the one thing Tracy's dad ever sent, he sent her this gold bracelet for her thirteenth birthday. But he didn't even buy *that* for her—he just found it on the beach. He's got one of them metal detectors. When Tracy pulled the bracelet out of the box, it still had sand on it."

"*It still had sand on it*?" Kimberly said.

Shelly nodded.

Laura looked back outside. Lightning bugs winked slowly across the lawn. Shelly's cat was pouncing after something small beneath an evergreen bush. Caesar was watching the cat but he didn't leave Tracy's side.

The girls watched in silence as Tracy finished her cigarette, put it out, and dropped it into a big gray ceramic birdbath.

Laura had extra room next to her because Tracy didn't return that night. Once the lights were off, there were a few short bursts of conversation, then the silence in between them grew longer and longer, and eventually she heard the heavy sounds of sleep around her.

Laura was so happy about the way the night had gone that she wasn't tired, even though it was nearly midnight. It seemed as though Shelly was going to invite her over again, that Shelly would be a friend at real school now too. Laura thought that would almost surely mean other new friends and maybe even an older boyfriend for her this fall.

She thought of Tracy's part-Indian boyfriend from Cheektowaga and wondered if he was over at Tracy's house right now, if that's why Tracy hadn't come back, if they were doing something bad while Tracy's mom was fast asleep because of the pills.

She wondered if Tracy's boyfriend knew the stuff about her dad, how he was out of the picture and sent her a bracelet that still had sand on it.

Laura pictured that piece of paper still resting upstairs on the kitchen counter with *Tracy's Allowance* written across the top. She pictured the list of dollar signs, the row of numbers doubling in size until they went the whole way across the stationary. She pictured a big chalkboard with those numbers, and she thought of how, if Tracy kept going, how fast those numbers would fill up a chalkboard. Then the numbers would fill a whole wall, a building, a block. The whole way across Lackawanna and over the lake, jumping across two states then four, soon so big they went beyond the planet Earth, doubling forever to infinity.

Laura tried to make her mind understand this. And as she thought about it more and more, she began to feel very grave and small and empty, like nothing was real and nothing mattered.

FORTY-DOLLAR CAB

Tracy invited Tom and Amelia out to her car for a smoke between the ceremony and the reception. She opened the sunroof manually. Amelia fanned her face with the wedding program as she watched an elderly couple exit the church, clutching one another's elbows down the stairs. The woman reached up to brush something from her husband's chin and he turned away from her, then swatted her hand when she went after it a second time. Her salmon pantsuit matched his pocket square. The ryegrass was brown and crisp. The Buffalo summer had come soaring in hot and it wasn't letting up.

"Tommy says you've got a kid," Tracy said, finding Amelia's eyes in the rearview mirror. Tracy had a dark, wild face and she was wearing a dress that was way too short for a wedding. She was nineteen years old. She had a strong way about her, despite bad posture.

Amelia stared at the back of Tom's head for a second—not even his own mother was allowed to call him *Tommy*. He and Tracy, second cousins, had grown up on the same street, but hadn't seen each other in almost a year, Tom said, since Tracy had moved to Florida for cosmetology school.

"Show her one of those with the floppy hat," Tom said over his shoulder.

Amelia pulled a picture from her wallet. She tapped Tracy on the arm with it.

"Cute," Tracy said, glancing at the picture but not reaching for it. She exhaled upward then passed the joint over her head to Amelia in the backseat. Flakes of white ash drifted like snow to Amelia's knee. She held the joint for a few seconds then handed it up to Tom. She felt a drop of sweat run from her armpit, cool down her side.

"Nice ceremony, huh?" Tom said. "I can't believe Chris is a *married man*."

"You wouldn't believe the way Chris used to terrorize me and Tommy," Tracy said. "He was such a pervert." The joint was thin between her lips and she spoke out of one corner of her mouth. "Remember the time he gave us five dollars to kiss?"

"Shut up, Tracy," Tom said. He turned to Amelia. "She's just trying to get a rise."

Tracy laughed like a shout then lowered her seat until she was practically in Amelia's lap.

"I'm just kidding, of course," Tracy said. She blinked up at the sky through the sunroof, and swung her open palm lazily at a fly that circled the car.

Amelia tried to gauge the length and loudness of her own laughter to match Tracy's, and she shifted her face out of the sunlight. A year after pregnancy, the bridge of her nose was still mottled with those curious gray-brown smears that her dermatologist called "melasma." He said the spots would fade with time, especially if Amelia stayed out of the sun and used the right products. She couldn't afford the lotion he had prescribed.

Tom asked Tracy if she was good to drive.

After the cake-cutting, Amelia sipped a glass of champagne and dissected a stale little profiterole with a toothpick while she watched Tom and Tracy spin across the faux-wooden dance floor. It was scratched and gleaming beneath them, like an ice rink. The cousins were both great dancers, funny and brave. They knew the lyrics and sang intensely to one another while aunts and uncles took pictures and brought them fresh drinks.

When they returned to the table, Tracy pried her shoes off and propped her bare feet up on an empty chair. Amelia could see a diamond of black underwear between Tracy's legs. There was no cellulite on the back of her thighs.

"Shelly got so tall," Tracy said, still panting. "Didn't she?"

"She's another cousin," Tom explained to Amelia, and pointed her out across the room.

"Shelly was so annoying," Tracy said, turning to Amelia. "She was such an attention hog. Always telling crazy stories that were no-way true. And she'd hide in the basement, just to point out how long it took anyone to notice. Anyway, this one time me and Tommy tied her to a tree and blindfolded her and pretended we were going to leave her there all night long."

"Geez," Amelia said. "You guys were rough on each other."

The bride and groom stopped by the table a moment later to greet the guests, and Tracy asked the bride if the flowers in the centerpiece had been spray-painted. Amelia coughed and stared intently across the room.

The burgundy carpet of the banquet hall was blackened and matted flat in heavily trafficked areas; the entrance to the kitchen, the path in front of the buffet station. Mirrors in bronze frames lined the walls, and the one nearest their table was slightly warped. Tom had snagged a bottle of champagne and he quickly refilled all of their flutes.

"I'm only gonna say it once," Tracy said after the newlyweds had moved on to the next table. "I think Chris could do better."

"She's all right," Tom shrugged.

Tracy had an iced tea in front of her. She took a Sweet'N Low packet from a little glass box and shook it by its corner before tearing into it. "I liked that last girl he was with a lot more."

Amelia wondered what Tracy thought of Tom's last girlfriend.

Amelia slipped out to the lobby to call her mother at nine o'clock.

Everything had gone just fine, her mother said, Casey was already asleep.

"I wanted to say 'night," Amelia said.

"I can wake her if you want me to."

"Nah." Amelia curled the cord around her index finger.

"How's the party?"

"It's good," Amelia said. "Did it take her a while to fall asleep?"

"Nope, we didn't even make it through all the books you left."

"Oh . . ." Amelia licked a spot of whipped cream from the outside of her hand. "I was afraid she might have trouble. Did she eat enough for dinner?"

"She ate plenty. Everything's fine, quit your worrying and we'll see you in the morning."

Amelia hung up the phone and stepped outside. A few of the groomsmen were smoking cigarettes by the dumpster. Their ties were loose and one of them was wearing aviator sunglasses on a chain around his neck. The wooded area beyond the lot was winking with fireflies. A mile or two up the shore, Amelia could make out the eight enormous white wind turbines that powered half of Lackawanna. She'd never before seen all of the windmills completely still, their limbs at rest in odd angles to one another. The air purred with nocturnal insects.

Inside, Tom said, "Everything OK?"

"She had some trouble getting to sleep without me, but . . . I think everything's good."

Tom looked at Tracy. "She always does this."

"What do I do?" Amelia said.

"What does she do?" Tracy said.

"You worry."

"Oh." Amelia smiled softly, bravely.

At midnight, the three of them retrieved their overnight bags from the coat check and split a cab downtown.

"Are you staying at the Embassy Suites too?" Amelia said.

"No," Tracy said. "My friend lives a block or two away, I'll crash at her place."

When Tracy got out of the cab, Tom said, "She's a hoot, isn't she? I knew you'd love her."

"She sure likes to make people squirm."

"You're the only one that's squirming." Tom poked Amelia in the side.

There were two identical beach paintings in their hotel room. One hung over the bed, and the other above the desk, where a phone book sat next to a pad of stationary and a wire cup of navy pens. Two thin terrycloth robes were folded neatly on the luggage rack.

Amelia went into the bathroom. Her hair was heavy with product so she pulled it back into a ponytail. She wrestled her dress off over her head and looked at herself in the full-body mirror. She didn't take off her heels. She adjusted her breasts within her bra so they were symmetrical.

They had been dating for several months, but since Tom had roommates and Amelia had her daughter, the only sex they'd had so far was brief and silent and in broad daylight. Tom had always touched her with the utmost caution and restraint, and Amelia wondered what it was about her that seemed so breakable. She wondered how he described her to his friends. She thought of the girl she'd accidentally encountered on a magazine in Tom's desk once when he was out of the room. She tried to arrange that girl's slinky, daring expression on her own face, but it didn't sit right.

When she peeked around the bathroom door, she saw that Tom was lying on the bed with his legs crossed and a sports show on mute. She stepped out of the bathroom with one slow, long stride. She had trouble keeping her balance on one heel and fought the surge of nervous, little-girl laughter that pumped in her chest.

"Look at you," Tom said, digging his fists into the bed and sitting up straight.

He ran his warm nose along her collarbone. She sighed in a small, urgent voice. The hotel phone on the bedside table rang. Tom made a face at it and turned back to Amelia. He worked at the clasp of her bra.

The phone rang again, and a moment later, a third time.

Tom said, "*Come on*," as he pulled away from Amelia to answer the phone. "Uh-huh," he said into the receiver, his hands on Amelia's hips, shoulder cradling the phone to his ear. "Uh-huh, OK, no problem." He hung up the phone.

"Tracy's friend isn't home and she's locked out of the place," he said, bringing his hands to his lap. He sighed. "She's downstairs in the lobby with a six-pack."

Amelia looked down at the comforter and ran her finger in a slow circle over the pattern.

"Sorry, hon," he said. "I'll make sure she doesn't stay long. I just feel bad, she's got no place to go, her mom isn't answering her calls . . ."

"No, of course," Amelia said. "Of course."

She wiggled back into her dress and needed his help with the zipper.

• • •

Tracy arranged herself across the pillows at the head of the bed, her tanned legs tossed out over the comforter. She had a black scab on her knee. She pulled the Coors Lights from a crinkled deli bag and handed one to both of them.

"Hey, you have something here," Tracy said, leaning toward Amelia and pointing at the bridge of her own nose.

Amelia flushed immediately and covered her face with her whole palm. "It's a skin thing," she said. "A condition. From when I was pregnant."

"Oh, sorry," Tracy said. "I noticed it earlier, it looks different in this light."

Tom cleared his throat and put his hand on Amelia's knee.

"How'd you come up with Cassie, anyway?" Tracy said.

"What?"

"Your daughter. Is she named after somebody?"

"It's Casey," Tom corrected her before Amelia could.

"No, it's not a family name or anything." Amelia's dress felt hot and tight. "I just like it."

Tracy took a sip of her beer. "I hate Florida," she announced. "I've got like no friends."

"You should move back here," Tom nodded emphatically.

Tracy drank three beers by herself while she talked about how lonely she was in Tallahassee, how much she missed Buffalo. How much she'd like to see her father, if only she could afford to go up to Michigan.

Amelia wondered how this girl rationalized and spoke so easily around what seemed obvious; that her parents were *bad* parents who made no effort to see or look after her. Tracy spoke about these things openly and with a casual thoughtlessness, as though she might bare her entire soul by accident, although she never shed a tear. Amelia was starting to recognize the gulf between people with parents like her own, parents who *worried*, and people with parents like these. She wished she was home with her own mother and her own daughter.

"How's your mom, anyway, Trace?" Tom said. "I haven't seen her in a while. Why wasn't she at the wedding?"

"She probably overslept," Tracy said. "She forgot to pick me up at the airport Friday. I had to take a forty-dollar cab."

"Geez," Tom said.

Tracy sank back into the pillows. The overhead light was off and a single lamp made the room soft and gold. She put her arms in the air and swayed them back and forth to the music of the commercial on TV. Her hair had collected sweat at the tips and it was heavy across her forehead. Amelia pulled the rubber band from her own hair and put it around her wrist. She wondered how bad the ponytail crease was.

Tracy picked up the phone at the bedside table and held it to her face. "Should we order a bottle of wine from room service, or what?" She nodded at the beer between her legs. "This is the last one."

Tom squinted at the digital clock.

"Come *on*, Tommy," Tracy twisted and untwisted the cord between her fingers. "When's the last time we hung out?" She puffed out her bottom lip and blinked fast.

Tom sighed. He didn't look at Amelia. "All right," he said to Tracy. "Cool your jets. All right, all right. Get the cheapest red."

Amelia went to the bathroom while Tracy made the call. When she turned off the faucet, she noticed that it was silent in the other room except for the low hum and game-show voices on the TV. She went to the wall and pressed her face against it. The tile was cool on her cheek. She didn't breathe. The wall sounded vast and lonesome at her ear, like a conch shell.

Amelia's own cousin Ray was four years older than her and they had kissed on the mouth once at Christmas when she was ten. He'd acted like he wanted to do more but she couldn't stop laughing, which made him mad.

Amelia opened the door. Tom was stretched on his back across the foot of the bed and his eyes were closed, his fingers crossed at his chest.

"I'm gonna get a cab," Amelia whispered to Tracy. "I think Casey's probably having trouble sleeping, she always does when I'm not there."

Tracy's mouth sagged open with a yawn. Her dress was hiked up around her waist and she held the beer between her thighs, right against her crotch.

"It's none of my business . . ." Tracy said. "But I think you've gotta toughen a kid up, you know? Or they'll turn out too soft." She stared at the scab on her knee then peeled up the corner of it with her fingernail.

Amelia picked up her purse.

"I'm serious," Tracy continued. "I think sometimes a kid just has to learn stuff the hard way." She ran her index finger around the lip of her beer. "My mom always says how when I was little, she'd let me bawl for hours and hours every single night, alone in my crib, so I'd learn to put myself to sleep. And eventually I did."

Amelia thought about what Tracy had said earlier. She pictured Tracy at the airport on Friday, and wondered how long Tracy had sat waiting for her mother to pick her up before realizing that she wasn't coming.

Tracy pulled the bottle out from between her legs and it squeaked across her skin. She finished the beer in one swallow. She blinked slowly and only one of her eyes reopened. "Later," she said, saluting Amelia slowly with two fingers.

Amelia gave Tracy a little wave and crept across the room barefoot with her bag over one shoulder and the straps of her shoes dangling from her index finger.

Tom stirred when she opened the door. "Are you leaving?" he lifted his chin half an inch to scowl at Amelia, then he turned to Tracy.

"She always does this," he said.

THE SPLASH ZONE

SeaWorld of Aurora, Ohio, was a bright, dusty, screaming place. Charlie was wearing a visor with tiny silver dolphins embedded in the cobalt blue foam. Jim suspected it was a gift from his ex-wife Laura's new boyfriend, who she had described as "imaginative." Jim hadn't met the guy.

Jim and Charlie stared at a three-dimensional map of the place, which offered auditory descriptions of each exhibit if you pressed the corresponding button. Hard plastic sea creatures blinked and vibrated and spoke if you turned them like a knob; a penguin, a walrus, an otter whose head looked gnawed on. Jim and Charlie listened to them all and double-checked the times of the Shamu show, which Charlie wanted to save for last. He wanted to get there at least half an hour, no, maybe a whole hour early so they would be guaranteed seats in the Splash Zone.

Jim didn't particularly want to be in the Splash Zone. He didn't have towels in the car to protect his leather seats for the long drive home. He couldn't really afford that car but had gotten a good deal since he worked at the dealership. He was also irritated to note that Charlie, like his mother, was already becoming a stickler on time. Laura had been a tyrant when it came to punctuality. Even before they were married, she would get all silent and uppity with Jim if he kept her waiting so much as five minutes.

He asked Charlie where he wanted to start.

"Sharks," Charlie said, then he scowled up at his father. "Dad, you didn't even notice." He threw his head back and jutted his lower jaw out into the sunshine.

"Lost your first tooth, did you?" Jim said.

"Wanna feel it?" Charlie grabbed Jim's index finger and put it into his mouth. It was hot and airless in there. Charlie guided the tip of his father's finger to the empty space.

"Did it hurt?" Jim asked. He pulled his finger out of Charlie's mouth and wiped it on his thigh.

"No," Charlie said, "but it bled a ton."

On their way to the shark tank, they passed a girl handing out water-soluble tattoos from a little blue pail. She was wearing way too much makeup for eleven o'clock in the morning, and a shirt that sat precariously on the corners of her slim shoulders. Jim wondered about the logistics of a bra, the likelihood that she was wearing one.

"You want one of those tattoos?" he asked Charlie.

The girl had a black spike through her eyebrow and she itched her face around it while Charlie sifted through the bucket. Jim couldn't think of a single thing to say to her. She looked vaguely hungover, like she probably didn't want to talk weather, or whales. Her arms were as skinny and shapeless as noodles.

Charlie settled on a Shamu tattoo, and Jim knelt to apply it. He was instantly pained by the familiar soupy smell of their house that clung to Charlie's shirt. The studio loft where Jim now lived by himself smelled inky and hygienic, like a place with too many rules. He peeled off the thin cover of the tattoo, licked his thumb, and smoothed the colored print over Charlie's cheek. He held it there for a few seconds, palming Charlie's skull in order to press the thing on nice and tight. He listened to a far-off megaphone crackle and broadcast an Australian guy going on about conservation.

Charlie examined his reflection in a nearby soda machine.

"Cool. Very cool. I want you to have one too," he said, so Jim got a second tattoo and applied it to his own cheek.

The shark tank surrounded a long, narrow viewing tunnel with glass lining the sides and overhead. An eerie, hollow drone played over the intercom—it was like stepping inside one of those seashells you hold up to your ear. The lighting was a cool and dark artificial green.

Sharks drifted by on both sides and loomed above them, looking bored and smug and well fed. A toddler shrieked and pounded the glass right in front of a tiger shark. The thing didn't give a shit.

Midway through the tunnel, they reached a massive jawbone mounted on a stainless-steel base. The bone was at least three feet across and gaping open nearly as tall as it was wide. Gleaming silver screws held it together at the corner hinges. The bone was yellowy gray, like an old baseball. The largest center teeth were as big as spearheads. Jim watched another dad put his head through the jawbone and make terrible faces like he was getting eaten, while his kids on either side of him squealed and pulled on his arms. Charlie was watching too, looking like he wanted to be in on the fun.

A freckled girl with a long blond braid stood next to the jawbone, holding a stack of pamphlets on the great white's status as an endangered species. She wore a light blue polo shirt with a shark embroidered on the collar. She brushed her cheek gently with the loose end of her braid.

Jim stepped forward to take a closer look at the bone and he noticed an empty spot along the bottom row of teeth. He ran his finger along that smooth pocket.

"Look here," Jim said to Charlie, "he's missing one just like you. Hey, did you put that tooth under your pillow?"

"Nah, I don't believe in fairies," Charlie said.

"What'd you do with it?" Jim absently stroked the jawbone then placed his whole palm over it.

"Kevin has it."

Jim stared at his son.

"Mom's new friend Kevin," Charlie explained.

"Yeah, I know who *Kevin* is," Jim said. "What the hell sort of business does Kevin have with your tooth?"

"We were at his house when it came out. I was eating a granola bar." Charlie's voice shrank with each word. "He cleaned the blood off and put it in a little bowl. It's in my room there."

Jim pictured Charlie's tooth, tiny and perfect like a little pearl sliced in half, the root as delicate as an eggshell.

He thought of the small wooden box where he'd kept all of his own baby teeth when he was a boy. The inside of the box was lined with burgundy velvet. Sometimes, he remembered, he'd take his teeth out of that box and arrange them on the floor in the shape of a jaw, to try and recreate the skeleton of his own mouth in the carpet before him.

Then Jim pictured the tooth sitting in this bowl in Kevin's house. Kevin's house, where Charlie evidently had his own bedroom. Kevin's house, where Kevin was doing God only knew what sorts of imaginative things to Jim's ex-wife at that very moment.

"Sir," the girl in the polo shirt stepped toward Jim and gave him an ominous look. "Sir, you can't touch that," she said. She pointed at a small bronze plaque that read "Please Do Not Touch."

Jim looked down and realized he was gripping the shark's jaw in a hard fist like he was about to rip the whole thing off the steel base. He didn't let go. A woman standing nearby moved slowly to position herself between Jim and her stroller. A plushy Cleveland Browns throw blanket covered the contents of the stroller entirely.

Jim wondered how much force it would take to free the jawbone. He wondered how thick the glass of the tank was—how hard it would be to fill that whole tunnel with a rush of rancid salted water and confused sharks. He felt his own face cycling through a series of wild and careless expressions. He was slick and cool with sweat.

"Sir, please let go of that bone," the girl said. She was scared now. Her voice sounded like something small getting the life squeezed out of it.

Jim suddenly remembered that he had a tiny blue smiling whale on his cheek. He let go of the jawbone and stepped backward. He held up his hand and examined the white crescents that the teeth had left smarting on his palm.

Jim was surprised to discover that beer was available at the food court. Half an inch of foam twinkled and spat at the surface of his Coors Light. He drank two-thirds of the beer while the cashier was still counting out change. The kid wore a Cleveland Indians cap covered with dozens of metal pins. Jim tipped him three dollars.

"Go Tribe," Jim said, and offered the kid a high five. He felt a hundred times better than he had moments earlier.

Charlie was licking his corndog like a popsicle and he had a smear of wet cornmeal on his chin. He eyed his father. "I thought you said you were getting a Coke."

"I thought that would be the only option," Jim said.

Charlie sighed with his entire upper body. He tapped the toe of his flip-flop irritably, like he was waiting on something. A sudden, cruel smirk passed over his face. "I'll probably have to tell Mom," he said.

"Great," Jim said. He gave Charlie a big thumbs-up. "*Perfecto mundo.*" He took another sip of his beer. "You have food on your face."

They walked to a nearby table shaded by a navy Pepsi umbrella. Charlie finished his corndog, then he poked the empty wooden stick methodically through the holes in the dark green plastic grating of the table. He adjusted his visor lower on his forehead.

"Tell Mom whatever you want to tell Mom," Jim said, finishing off the beer. He ran his index finger around the rim of the plastic cup to capture the residual foam and sucked it off his fingertip. He gazed across the pavilion at a large man who was shading himself with an umbrella and stroking a Pomeranian on his lap.

"Maybe I won't," Charlie said quietly and glanced sideways at Jim.

"I don't suppose Kevin ever drinks a beer," Jim said.

"Not really," Charlie said. "Sometimes he has a wine."

Jim crushed the empty plastic cup in his hand. He wanted another one. Ten more.

He knew he deserved all of this.

Six months after the finalization of their divorce, Laura was still on the lookout for ways to finagle the other woman into conversation, even hinting at it when Charlie was around. Jim had recently convinced himself for several terrible hours that she'd told Charlie, who was particularly sour during an outing. Laura hadn't, she later insisted, but Jim knew that she would. She would wait until Charlie was old enough to understand, old enough to decide for himself what kind of a man his father really was, Jim was certain of this. Already, Jim felt his son's judgment and the widening gulf between them, father and son hurtling away from each other at some invisible velocity.

Charlie went to the bathroom, and Jim stared absently at a teenage couple as they ate fries with melted cheese from a cardboard box, a graceful orange string accompanying each bite. An enormous inflatable dolphin was propped up in the seat next to the girl. Jim wondered if the kid had won it for her in some game, or actually paid money for that thing.

Jim spun self-consciously back toward the men's room. His sunglasses hung from a string around his neck, and he wiped the lenses off with the bottom of his shirt then looked at his reflection in them. His nose was thick and sunburned and porous, lips chapped to crusts in the corners, eyes soggy-looking and threaded with tired blood.

Laura's face was so beautiful that even when they were still together, it sometimes made Jim mad to look at her. Somewhere inside himself he had always known that she was too good, that it would turn out this way.

Jim put his sunglasses back on and raised his arm at Charlie who was walking out of the men's room still clutching a balled-up paper towel. Jim knelt to pick up the clear plastic lid of a fountain soda cup off the ground, and he threw it like a Frisbee into the garbage can several feet away. He pulled a small tube of SPF 45 from his pocket and rubbed the pasty goo onto Charlie's face and arms and bare little legs.

Jim and Charlie wore plastic gloves while they tossed handfuls of glittering fish to barking sea lions. They took pictures of a diseased-looking walrus, its flesh mottled pink around its face. They watched a row of penguins zoom down a slide, flipping head over heels into water that was outlandishly blue. They passed a small pond with a fountain that was full of mallards, their green heads resplendent in the midday sun. Jim watched as Charlie approached the pond and leaned over it. He had his eye on something beneath the surface, and when Jim joined him, Charlie pointed. Several feet out in the water was a tiny baby turtle, its shell no more than two or three inches long, and it was swimming furiously against an artificial current that was being created by the fountain. On the far side of the fountain was a rock where five or six other turtles lay in the sun. The tiny turtle, for all his efforts, couldn't seem to get beyond the fountain to join the others on the rock. His little legs churned. Each time he'd make a bit of progress or attempt a different route, the strength of the water would overtake him and send him tumbling backward.

Jim said, "He doesn't know what he's up against, does he?"

At the far end of the pond, a kid in a latex seal mask howled at them.

At four o'clock, they made their way over to the main auditorium for the Shamu show. Cement semicircular tiers rose back from the pool, which was surrounded by a four-foot-tall panel of glass. The first twelve rows were marked "Splash Zone," the lettering in blue spray paint with a faint blue rectangular outline of the stencil visible around each word. Jim followed Charlie to two open seats several rows back, at center stage. A vendor carried a wicker basket full of football-sized stuffed whales. He wore his SeaWorld hat backward on his head and his khaki shorts were frayed to strings at his knees. A whale in both his hands, pantomiming some fight scene. A few rows down, there was a little boy wearing a girl's wig. A pair of twins that looked to be about Charlie's age sat in front of Jim and passed a white paper bag of popcorn back and forth. One of them hurled a single piece of popcorn into the pool when their mother wasn't watching, and Jim watched it soften in the water.

Jim had a camping trip planned with Charlie for Labor Day weekend. They would go to Cattaraugus Creek, just an hour outside Buffalo. Fish during the daytime, swim if the sun was shining, roast hotdogs at night, read stories in the tent with a flashlight. The trip had been planned for several months now, but suddenly Jim felt nothing but bitterness about the whole scenario; certain that Laura had some great big plan with Kevin for that long weekend. St. Croix, perhaps, or some other saintly island. And what would he and Charlie even talk about for three whole days? At this moment, he couldn't think of a single thing he ought to say to this boy, a single question he could ask. He looked at Charlie, who was tracing circles on his kneecap with his index finger. *Three days* together?! An eternity.

The show began with gentle music and an informational video about killer whales, which was projected on the far screen behind the pool. Jim wished there was a beer vendor, like at baseball games. When the video ended, the screen rose upward out of sight, and a girl in a wetsuit trotted out around the perimeter of the pool, chirping into her microphone. Her wetsuit was like a second skin of glistening black, and even from a distance, Jim could see every angle and detail of her athletic body within it, including the delicate, happy point of her small nipples. He wondered how shriveled everything was when she squeezed out of that wetsuit at the end of a shift, how long its seams stayed imprinted on her flesh.

The whale finally appeared at the far left side of the pool, its gleaming black snout first. It glided to the center of the pool, fully submerged but visible through the glass, its tail sweeping left and right, creating a gentle slithering current that reached the water's surface. At center stage, the whale rose to the surface, turned onto its back, and reached one of its huge paddle-like flippers up and out of the water in a lazy wave toward the audience. Its belly was as smooth and white as cream. It rolled back onto its stomach, and its exposed blowhole hissed and wheezed. Jim was impressed by the size of the whale, the precise and pleasing symmetry of its blacks and whites. Big white oval eyespots made the whale look very kind and not quite real.

The girl in the wetsuit reached into a metal bucket to pull out a wriggling ten-inch-long fish by its tail. She dropped the fish directly into the whale's smile and it barely twitched to swallow the fish whole, then several more.

The girl dove in and out of the water for several tricks, at one point jogging in place on the whale's belly while it swept slowly across the pool. The girl hugged its snout, disappeared with it under the water and reemerged straddling its dorsal fin. She hopped off the whale and onto the stage, and rewarded it with more fish.

"All right," the girl said, undoing and redoing her slick wet ponytail and adjusting her mouthpiece. "Those of you in the Splash Zone had better move back now if you don't wanna get wet."

The whale disappeared to its private pool behind the stage, the arena lighting dimmed, and the music faded to a deep, foreboding hum.

The twins in front of Jim poked one another. Their young mom covered her hairdo with her forearms. Charlie bounced in his seat. The whale appeared once again at stage left and swooped across the pool underwater. Three times the whale circled, picking up speed, and on its fourth pass, the music swelled to a percussive climax. When the whale reached center stage, neon strobe lights swirled wildly around the arena, and the whale disappeared deep into the pool.

The girl started a countdown from ten and invited the audience to join her. When they reached "*one!*" the whale exploded straight up out of the water. At the peak of its jump, it arched backward in the air, straightening its body so it was parallel to the water's surface, forked tail curled upward, flippers outstretched. Charlie gasped and threw his arms around his father. His whole face was wide open and his tiny biceps felt like bike tires pumped too tight.

Jim wondered when would be the next time his son reached for him like this, and when would be the last. He felt a private, throbbing panic.

The whale crashed down with a huge, graceful swell of water and for a moment, everything felt slow and slippery and just out of reach, like the end of a dream. The water stretched and oozed and reshaped itself like an enormous line of cursive before scattering in the air. The audience screamed and winced collectively. Charlie let go of Jim just in time to grab his visor off his head and clutch it protectively in his lap.

He shrieked when the water struck.

It hit hard and it was cold. It took Jim's breath away for a moment, as though he'd been slapped. He shivered vigorously from the base of his spine. He took a few shallow breaths and rubbed his eyes. Everyone around him was applauding. He blinked. The contact lens in his left eye had shifted and it now swam uncomfortably high on his eyeball, too far up to capture with his fingertip. Jim pulled his lid out and snapped it back, rolling his eye up far and wide in an attempt to locate it.

His chest was soaked. He could smell the fishy filth of the water, even through the chemicals. He couldn't get his vision to focus. The misplaced contact lens felt as big and as bad as a sheet of paper stuffed into his eye socket. It made him need to cough and sneeze.

"Charlie? Are you OK?" Jim reached for Charlie, and when he found his knee he cupped it in his left hand. He couldn't tell which of them was shaking.

"Whew-ie!" the girl was laughing loud and fake into her microphone, like a talk-show host. Jim searched for Charlie's face, but couldn't find it through the gluey blur of his left eye.

"Whew-ie!" the girl said again. "Y'all survive that?"

Jim rubbed his eye hard with the heel of his hand. Finally, the contact slid back onto his eyeball with smooth and satisfying adherence. He blinked and peered down at Charlie, who was smiling wide enough for Jim to see the gap of his missing tooth.

Charlie reached into his pocket and produced a small black comb. He parted his hair and combed through it. Then he put the comb back in his pocket and returned the visor to his head, straightening it. Jim gazed at his son curiously while he did these things, as though Charlie was a friend of a friend who Jim couldn't quite place.

Jim wrung out the front of his shirt with a fist, and reached for his wallet to make sure his cash hadn't been soaked. His eyeball stung something awful and now it was watering, his vision corrugated. He wiped his face with the back of his wrist and braced himself for the next big splash.

SOUTHTOWNS

Christopher Green introduced himself as "Greenie." He was only twenty-five, though a mature twenty-five, and Tracy a youthful thirty-nine. Greenie spiked his black hair up in the front and flattened the rest of it to his skull with gel. He had a small square patch of hair beneath his lower lip. His eyes were the thinnest, palest blue, a shade best suited to watercolor. He wore loads of cologne and crunched through an entire tin of Altoids in a shift, to cover up the smell of the cigarettes that he smoked every hour on the hour. He wasn't snooty like the rest of the staff, who talked about wine like they knew what they were talking about.

Tracy and Greenie were the only two staff members who drove into work from the Southtowns, the cluster of suburbs south of the city, rather than walking from an apartment downtown, and when she discovered this on his fourth day at the restaurant, she suggested that they carpool on the days they worked together.

"I'll drive tomorrow," she said. "They're calling for a foot overnight and I just got my tire chains put on."

It was a wet, smeary snow. Tracy's wipers ticked and squealed back and forth, thick icy logs collecting at the base of her windshield. The streets were splashy and translucent with slush. As she braked for a lineup at the 290 exit, she was met by the familiar smell of toasting Cheerios. She peered out her window. Black smoke gushed upward in steady huffing columns from the central wing of the sprawling General Mills plant. Between soaring smokestacks, a grain elevator had the giant orange General Mills *G* blazed on the highest tier of its white tower.

The plant occupied almost a half mile of Lake Erie shoreline. Folks were always fussing about the pollution, proximity to downtown, wasted lakefront property. Tracy didn't give much of a crap about stuff like this, local politics. She wondered what Greenie thought about these things, and the black man who was recently elected mayor.

She took Route 5, which ran along the water. The unfrozen lake was charcoal colored and wrinkled up against the snow-covered shore. A cyclone of little black birds danced in the wind.

When Tracy reached Greenie's house, she was surprised to learn that he still lived with his parents. It was a plain little split-level home that sat out near the road, yellow with blue shutters. A few tall maples, bare and black, rose on either side of the house, and there was a Rubbermaid mailbox at the mouth of the driveway. A basketball hoop hung above the garage, the net gray and torn long.

"I'm looking for a place," Greenie said, stepping up into Tracy's truck. He waved at his dad who was wearing a Buffalo Sabres ski hat and khaki overalls and pushing a wide shovel across the driveway. Tracy waved at his dad too.

"I've got my eye on a couple houses on Shorewood," Greenie continued, "some real fixer-uppers down that way. My old man did construction for a while."

"You'd buy it then?"

"My folks would help me out. I just haven't found the right place for the right price. I'd like something with a view of the lake."

"That's my thought too," Tracy said. "A view of the lake."

It was quiet for a bit, and then Tracy said, "I was into real estate for a while. Never got my certification, but I know a lot about it. I'll check out the listings for you, if you want."

They passed a boarded-up Blockbuster and a park with a tilted merry-go-round. She pointed out her house on the left. The neighborhood was nicer under cover of snow, she thought, when you couldn't make out the car parts and rusted barbecue sets and fat yellow Toys "R" Us kitchenettes that littered her neighbors' lawns. A soaring lake wind had swept the accumulated snow up into drifts with tips like meringue.

"Now you'll know where to find me," she said.

• • •

The next day, Tracy replaced the *Us Weeklys* she kept at her hostess stand with a stack of local papers and she spent the evening poring over the listings in search of fixer-uppers with a view of the lake. The dinner rush came and went. She had to remind the busboys to double-check the white linen tablecloths for stains before resetting on top of a dirty one. This wasn't the kind of a place where they could get away with dirty linens, she said. Get your act together. She liked the busboys, but they could be real dummies sometimes.

After the rush, she made her way over to the bar and asked Greenie for a Sprite. She pushed the stack of local papers across the bar.

"I highlighted some places," she said.

"You're a go-getter."

She sat at the bar and arranged her short black skirt at her thighs. She crossed her legs and spun once on the stool. It squeaked.

"We should replace these," she said. "I'm gonna bring it up with Chef."

Tracy was the only female on staff and she had an eye for detail. She liked making recommendations about the décor, even though none of these changes had ever actually gone into effect. The only other woman who had ever worked at the restaurant with Tracy was Chef's mother, Wanda, who used to come in on busy weekends to help out at the host stand. Wanda smelled like a Band-Aid and she was a real stick in the mud; once she had waited for Tracy as she washed her hands in the employee bathroom, then leaned into her and said, "Honey, you need to get a lather going. See, that, what you just did, that's not sanitary." Tracy wasn't entirely disappointed when Chef had announced that Wanda had a blood clot in her leg and wouldn't be working there anymore.

Tracy stayed at the bar and drank several more Sprites, leaving only to answer the phone for several reservations and to seat a few small parties. A purplish dusk appeared briefly, then it was dark, and then it was black.

Tracy helped Greenie light the candles, then she Windexed the whole bar and wiped it down while he did inventory on the wine. When she returned to her stool, he handed her something that didn't taste like Sprite.

"Little something extra in there for ya," he said.

"Is that vodka?" she said.

She sucked it down to ice quick before any of the servers came by.

"I used to work for Absolut," Tracy said, nodding at the bottle behind Greenie.

"Yeah?"

"I worked a few events for them," she explained. "I was gonna get into marketing, go corporate with them. But they wanted to relocate me. They wanted me to go to New York City." She spun an earring between her thumb and index finger. "But I said no can do. This was back when my mom was sick."

A drink ticket appeared on Greenie's machine and he ripped it off and speared it. He poured a martini for a server who came by for it a moment later.

Steve looked at the drink. "I said *up*, Greenie. Geez, man."

Greenie pulled the ticket back from the stack and examined it in front of a candle. "My fault. It'll just be a minute."

Tracy waited until Steve had disappeared into the kitchen then she spoke with a lowered voice, "Steve can be a real prick." She said it conspiratorially, leaning near to Greenie; it was her and him against the rest of them.

"These guys are real uptight," Greenie diplomatically agreed. "I don't know if I can hack this place."

"You'll get used to it. It can be funny sometimes."

Tracy told Greenie the story of the valet kid, who just a few weeks earlier had been tackled by several policemen while entering a BMW in the lot behind the restaurant, on Chippewa. The kid tried to tell the cops he was a restaurant employee entering the car legally, but the cops weren't buying it. They walked him into the restaurant in cuffs and Tracy had to vouch for him. They'd all had a good laugh about that.

Greenie laughed now too, and it was big and pleasant.

"See? You'll like it here," Tracy said, feeling triumphant. "Give it a little time."

She went to the bathroom. She kept a cosmetics case in the cabinet beneath the sink, behind the stacks of toilet paper. She pulled out her lipstick and applied it. Her hair was full and nicely highlighted. She did the highlights herself. The year after graduating high school, she'd done a semester of cosmetology school and still had a knack for color. She'd dyed her mother's grays a nice honey blond for nearly a decade until it had all fallen out.

Tracy brushed bronze eye shadow onto her brow bone. She had been at the restaurant for several years and often found guests to flirt with, but Greenie was the first staff member she cared to impress. He was too young, she knew that, young men weren't good to her, and for that matter she generally preferred married men. Or, not necessarily the men themselves, but the victory in it, the validation. But Greenie was something new. Beneath those muscles and the spiked hair there were eyes that were so pale and soft. There was someone in there who seemed a bit unsure of himself, a bit lonely in a nice way.

Tracy returned to the bar.

Greenie poured her another drink and when he handed it to her he winked with his whole face.

"What'd you say you studied in school again, Greenie?"

"Sports management." He balled up a bar rag and threw it toward a garbage can at the other end of the bar. It loosened in the air and landed with a flop several inches shy of the can. Tracy liked how he moved. She swung her feet from the stool and let the backs of her shoes fall free from her heels.

"I thought about doing something in sports too for a while," she said. "Broadcasting."

"Oh?"

"I took a class in it. My teacher said I had the right look. It would have been weird hours though, like really early mornings sometimes." She split her ponytail between her two hands and pulled to tighten it.

"What sports do you do?" she said.

"Nothing serious anymore, but I did swimming and basketball. Captain of the swim team, three years in a row."

"I never learned how to swim," Tracy said. She blew her nose into a cocktail napkin.

"Is that right?" Greenie said. "I thought everybody did swim lessons when they're little."

"Not I," said Tracy. "Maybe you can teach me."

Greenie smiled. She admired his teeth. A few too many for the size of his head, she thought, but all of them very straight and *very* white. She'd noticed this about others his age and wondered what the secret was.

In the kitchen, Tracy found Chef standing over a *Sports Illustrated* magazine and eating a ham sandwich. He was wearing a wrinkled and bloody white apron over a Bills jersey, and green kitchen scrubs. The collar of his jersey looked too tight around his neck and the lettering in the back was pale pink—Tracy guessed he had done his own laundry and washed the colors in hot. His black Crocs were dusted with flour and she could see the pale top of his feet through the ventilation holes.

Tracy tore a piece of bread from a loaf that had been sitting out and gone cool and hard. "Don't mind if I do." She dipped the crust straight into the soup kettle.

"You like that Greenie kid or something?" Chef said without looking up from the magazine.

"Nah," said Tracy.

She ate too much bread and felt less happy with her outfit.

The radio was on and the guys on 93.9 were between songs and weather advisories, talking football now. Over the weekend, the Bills had traded their second-string quarterback for a wide receiver, and everyone had their opinion about that. Tracy spun and walked out of the kitchen, the swinging doors crashing behind her before settling back into place. Sometimes the kitchen guys whistled at her, sometimes they didn't.

With only twenty minutes left until close, the restaurant was nearly empty and the servers had gathered at the bar to cash out when Tracy heard the jangle of bells at the front door.

She slid off her barstool and met four girls at the door. They wore tiny dresses beneath North Face coats. Tracy didn't offer menus right away.

"Four of you?" she said. She tried to stand wide between the girls and the bar so that Greenie wouldn't be able to see them. The petite black-haired girl had glitter on her cleavage. She said, "We just wanted to get one drink."

Tracy made a disapproving face. "We close in ten or fifteen, but there's a nice bar two blocks down and they're open later. They have fun cocktails, chocolate and stuff. We just have a really basic bar."

"That's fine," the girl said, then, "You trying to chase us off or something?" She wore the dumb, defiant expression of a six-year-old.

Tracy followed the girls to the bar and said, "Card them," to Greenie.

She went back to her hostess stand and watched Greenie pour drinks for the girls. She overheard him ask if they were students. They were, seniors at Buff State. Tracy didn't like the way they talked to Greenie; smiling big at his jokes, leaning their breasts all over the place, their laughter like metal on metal, the sharpening of blades. They talked about graduation and how they were all moving away after, for jobs in New York or Boston.

At eleven o'clock on the dot, Tracy lowered the volume of the music and she went to the bar and started to blow out the candles.

"*Kids*," she said after they'd left, giving Greenie a weary look, as though they could share this sentiment. "They don't have a clue, do they?"

"They left me a nice tip," Greenie said.

Something in Tracy smarted. "Probably all on Daddy's tab, you know those Buff State girls," she said. "I'll be out front when you're ready."

She smoked a cigarette while she waited for Greenie to close out. The air was dense with cold and dried salt crunched under her feet. The moon was low and thin. She pretended to be on her phone when she saw him approaching.

"Bills game is tied at halftime," she said, snapping her phone shut.

"Is that right?" Greenie said. "I might pop into a bar to catch the second half." He danced athletically on his toes, underdressed for the cold in just a gray hoodie over his work clothing. He pulled the hood over his head, arranged it at his cheeks. "*Oh*," he said quickly, "Scratch that, I don't want to make you wait til the game's over to drive me."

"You know," Tracy said, "I just got a flat-screen a few weeks ago. It hasn't gotten near enough use. A couple of my neighbors might come over to watch the end of the game and have a beer. You want to come?"

Greenie rocked the crown of his head back and forth within the hoodie.

"Or I could just run you home first." Tracy said casually. She ran her tongue over her lips and followed Greenie's gaze across Chippewa. Neon pinks and greens lit the entrance of Venue. The girls from the bar were midway through a line of people waiting to enter the club. A man stomped and clapped his gloves together behind his smoking soft pretzel cart. An airplane inched across the night sky, winking red.

"Do whatever you want," Tracy said. She reached into her purse for another cigarette.

"I'll come over," Greenie said.

"Whiskey or beer?" she called from her kitchen.

"Whichever you're having," he said.

Tracy hoped he didn't notice the smell in her house. She had run the vacuum sweeper that morning. There was something rank and rotting in her vacuum and it made the house stink like a dairy farm every time she swept. She kept meaning to replace the bag and clean the nozzle. Well, at least the carpet looked clean, anyway. She stared at the door of her refrigerator and pulled down a magnet from a friend that said: "I'm Like Fine Wine: Aged, Sophisticated, and Full-Bodied." Tracy glared at it in her palm then set it upside down on the counter. She centered the Polaroid of herself and her cousin Shelly, taken when they were children, their eyeballs soft and maroon in the old photograph.

She brought a bottle of whiskey out with two tumblers and set them on the coffee table. The radiator in the corner hissed and spat a rusty vapor into the room as it kicked on.

"My granddad played for the Bills," she said.

"That right? What'd he play?"

"Running back. He got his knee all tangled up at the start of his second season though, and never played again."

"So do you get to lots of games then?" Greenie said.

"No, I've never been."

"Really? Even with your granddad and everything?"

"Nah, he wasn't around much, and me and my mom couldn't afford it."

"It's a racket," Greenie agreed. "Fifty bucks for a nosebleed."

Tracy wondered if this meant he was one of those guys who suited up in Zumba pants, a jersey, and a foam finger just to watch games at home.

"I'm saving up to go, though," Tracy said. "Saving up for a seat at the lower-level sideline. I'm going next fall for my birthday. I figure if I'm gonna get to a game, I want the best seat in the house."

"How much do those run?"

"Six, eight hundred."

Greenie whistled softly through his teeth. "That's something else about your granddad. Too bad about the injury. What'd he do after that?"

Tracy said, "I don't know. Not too much of anything."

After the Bills won, the two of them did a celebratory shot, then another one for the hell of it.

"Your place is really big," Greenie said.

"Yeah, me and my mom shared it for a long time. It's the right size for two, too big for just little old me. I'm looking to buy a smaller place."

"Yeah," Greenie said. "The Southtowns are the pits."

"Oh, I'm not talking a different neighborhood. I don't aim to leave the Southtowns. Just buy a smaller place and use the extra money to open a business."

"Oh yeah?" Greenie was scrolling through the channel guide and didn't look away from the television.

"I wish I had something decent to offer you to eat," Tracy said. She had cooked a lot for her mother in those last few years, and their refrigerator was always full of rich, cheesy leftovers in a nine-by-thirteen pan. These days, Tracy ate strange little meals by herself above the sink; mayonnaise on crackers, cold pasta from a can, a stack of pepperoni.

"I'm gonna order from Paglio's," she said. "What toppings do you like and how much will you eat?"

Greenie wrestled his shoes off and put his feet up on the edge of the coffee table. His socks had a yellow line across the toe. "Sausage and green peppers. And I'm probably good for three pieces."

Tracy dialed the pizza place on her phone and while she was on hold she covered the mouthpiece and said to Greenie, "I'm not keeping you, am I? I could run you home right now."

"Nah," he said.

Once the pizza had been ordered, she refreshed his drink, then announced that she was going to take a shower.

"I hate smelling like restaurant," she said.

She tossed a towel over the bathroom linoleum where it was peeling up in the corner, exposing rows of mucus-yellow glue and rotting wood. Mildew bloomed across the ceiling, but there was nothing she could do about that. She hoped her shower wouldn't blare like a foghorn like it occasionally did when she first turned it on. After her shower, she put on a small pair of shorts and a tank top with no bra. She applied just a little bit of makeup, not enough that he would notice. She had the beginnings of one varicose vein on the back of her left knee. She spread a Band-Aid over it. She went out to the living room with her hair still dripping.

Greenie had finished his drink. She poured him another one and they ate pizza, then he pulled her tank top off over her head and stared at her breasts for a moment before touching them.

Tracy got on top. She watched herself in the reflection of the window. Greenie was very drunk. She pulled his hands up from where they rested beside him on the couch to place them at her waist so that it looked better.

He went to the bathroom afterward then said, "Do you mind if I check my email?"

She showed him to her desk in the dining room, where he parked his bare ass on the folding chair in front of her laptop. Tracy tried to sit on his lap, and he scooted the chair back to accommodate her.

"What happened to your leg?" He pointed at the Band-Aid.

"I cut myself shaving."

He clicked on her Internet browser, which immediately opened the job-aptitude website she'd been looking at earlier that day.

"What's this?"

"Nothing," she said. "Well . . . it's just this site that asks you a bunch of questions about yourself, your personality and stuff, and it tells you what you should be."

"What did it say you should be?"

"I didn't finish it yet."

Greenie opened a new window and checked his email. He signed out of his email account and signed into Facebook.

"You like that stuff?" she said.

"What, Facebook?" Greenie shrugged and scrolled through his newsfeed. He yawned into his fist. "Mind if I get something to drink?"

Tracy got off his lap. She followed him into the kitchen, where he stared into her refrigerator for a minute, then he reached for the gallon of milk and bottle of chocolate syrup. Tracy handed him a glass. Greenie squeezed a noisy black slurp of chocolate into a glass of milk and stirred up a muddy little tornado. He pointed at the rotary phone on the wall. "I didn't know people still had those."

"My mother's," Tracy said. "I just haven't gotten around to disconnecting the thing."

Greenie drank his milk quickly then returned to the couch and fell heavily onto it.

Tracy returned to her computer, reopened her job-aptitude test and finished the remaining questions. She clicked "Find Results" and waited a moment. A list appeared: "Administrative Assistant, Early Childhood Care, Shopkeeper, Bookkeeper, Customer Service."

Tracy went to the kitchen to pour herself some water and found that Greenie had spilled some of his chocolate milk on the linoleum. She wiped it up with her American flag dishtowel and ate a handful of Frosted Flakes.

At her computer, she closed the results window and refreshed the test. Perhaps, she thought, she didn't *always* adhere strictly to her routine; she could be spontaneous. She reached the section on creativity and considered her outfit from earlier; maybe she *did* have a strong sense of style.

She submitted the new set of answers and the "Results" window popped up a moment later: "Public Relations, Performing Arts, Arts Management, Interior Design, Fashion Design."

Tracy unplugged her laptop and took it to the living room. Most of the gel was gone from Greenie's hair and it was soft across his forehead. He slept with his lips parted and a sliver of one of his eyeballs was exposed through the lid. He was only wearing his boxers, and his thighs were thin and pale. Tracy faced the laptop toward him and brightened the screen.

"Hey, look what it says, Greenie," she said. She took his shoulder hard in her hand and shook it. "Look what this thing says I should be."

THE RICHEST HILL ON EARTH

Jim didn't care too much for Butte, with all those hills and the headframes that loomed over town like black skeletons. Unlike other mining towns, the operation in Butte had taken place in residential areas, and remnants of the industry could be found right outside the window of Jim's apartment. Rust and shadows and "No Trespassing" signs. He also didn't like the little Bert Mooney Airport that he'd flown into, with the greeter in a red suit who had practically forced a local chocolate upon him, but couldn't tell him the address of the nearest liquor store. Oh, and of course there was the nursing school located at the center of town, with the young students who wouldn't give Jim a second look, except when it was one of foreboding distaste. It seemed he'd reached an age where eye contact with an undergraduate was considered either a threat, or just plain laughable.

Jim had been transferred to the Decker Quality Foods plant here a month ago, with a big wave of new crewmembers. The assignment was lucrative, but temporary. Just this afternoon, another new batch of transplants had arrived. Friendly chaps from the Midwest. It had all put Jim in a really foul mood. These guys weren't like him. These guys were saving up to put a kid through college, and arrived with a wallet full of photographs. These were the kind of guys who found that airport greeter charming. These guys couldn't wait for the assignment to end so they could get back home. Jim didn't have a clue what he'd do when his contract ran out. He'd burned all his bridges prior to landing this job, didn't even know of a single couch he could crash on if it came to that.

The welcome dinner, a catered event in the basement cafeteria of the Decker Quality Foods plant, was served on plastic beneath fluorescent lights. The open bar was beer and wine only. The General Manager talked about teamwork and punctuality and he did a demonstration with the new safety goggles, showed how to adjust the grip to your head size.

Following the dinner, Jim found himself at the High Horse with a few whiskeys boiling in his stomach and another one on the bar before him. The rest of the Decker Food guys typically went out drinking to The Crystal, where they served all the local beers on draft. This is where the nursing students tended to hang out, where they did salsa nights, and karaoke on Thursdays.

Jim preferred the High Horse, a dark little haunt that smelled like grease and damp wood and poor plumbing. There were seldom more than half a dozen guys at the High Horse, and they all drank liquor, straight. Also, Jim was the only one who ever expressed a preference for the television channel, so he got to watch his hometown Buffalo Bills whenever there was a game. The bartender was a guy with a wolfish face and gray beard, and he didn't care to exchange any more words with the patrons than what was absolutely necessary for the transaction.

Jim was scowling at a commercial on TV advertising "no money down" for a brand-new Toyota Camry at the local dealership, when a guy leaned over the stool next to him, resting his elbows on it, and said, "You mind?"

Jim nodded toward the seat. "All yours."

Jim recognized the guy—they'd met earlier in the evening, at the welcome dinner. This guy had said that he was another transplant from the Dunkirk plant in New York, although Jim couldn't recall that they had ever crossed paths back there. The guy was tall and barrel-chested, seemed shy and pleasant enough, had a deep, earthy voice, and wore a handsome red flannel buttoned high. Long ponytail beneath a black, gambler-style cowboy hat. His face was weathered but handsome—strong angles, dark complexion, eyes that were either all iris or all pupil, and Jim guessed that he was Native American.

Earlier at the welcome dinner, they had stood next to one another at the bar. The guy had ordered an O'Doul's, and Jim had commented on it—said that he ought to be doing the same.

Now the guy settled into the stool next to Jim's, reached across the bar for a laminated menu stuck into the side of the condiment compartment tray, and stared at it. He put the menu back in its sleeve and tapped his right index finger slowly on the bar. When the bartender came over, the guy ordered coffee and a chicken-fried steak.

Jim said, "Didn't get enough slop at that company gig?"

"Didn't care too much for it."

"Me either," Jim said. "I'll be curious to know what you think of that chicken-fried steak. You know, I been in this town a month and have yet to get a decent meal. You believe they used to call this town the 'richest hill on earth'?"

The guy raised his eyebrows noncommittally.

Jim shoved his empty whiskey glass back toward the bar. "This is for sleepin' purposes," he explained to the guy, after ordering another.

The guy's coffee arrived and he opened a creamer into it, stirred slowly with the sharp end of a butter knife.

Jim was drunk and feeling uncharacteristically chatty. He liked this guy. He said, "You got family?"

The guy shook his head. "You?"

"Not particularly," said Jim. "Although . . ." He held his fresh whiskey in front of his eyes, tipped it back and forth and examined the oil-like patterns of gold swirling up and down the side of the glass, the slow disintegration of the ice, the subtle change in the drink's color. Two rocks, that's how he liked it, and they seldom melted in the time it took him to finish a drink. "I've got a kid."

They watched the TV in silence for a while.

The bartender appeared with the guy's chicken-fried steak and set it in front of him. Then, he handed him a bottle of ketchup and a steak knife wrapped in a paper napkin. The guy put the paper napkin on his knee and sawed into the steak. The steak was reddish and roughly textured, like a chunk off the planet Mars, and beside it were home fries that gleamed with grease and were speckled with dried herbs and black char.

"My kid's thirteen now," Jim offered. "Almost a man. Been raised by some other guy, a real piece of work, this guy." Jim shook his head. "Thing is, I can't even blame this other guy too much. I messed it all up before he even hit the scene—messed it up with his mom first, and then after we split, with my kid too."

Jim blinked, feeling this betrayal fresh and achy, like unexpected pressure on a deep bruise.

He watched the guy saw into the steak.

"Anyway," Jim said. "Kids don't forget some stuff."

Jim thought back to the last camping trip that he and his son had attempted, to Cattaraugus Creek on Labor Day weekend, following Jim and Laura's recent separation.

Jim and Charlie had arrived midmorning, pitched the tent, and fished for several hours. Jim explained to his son that Cattaraugus meant "foul-smelling river," and it was given the name because of the natural gases it oozed, but, he said, the smell wasn't too bad this time of year. Charlie disagreed. He said it smelled like a skunk's butt. After lunch and a nap, Charlie was ready to go home, but Jim informed him that this was not in the plans. Jim had already made all the arrangements to spend two days and two nights on the river. He had packed enough food and bait, a few games and a stack of books for Charlie, some special sugary snacks.

They fished for another hour or two in the afternoon, then fought before dinner, as Jim started to make preparations for the night. Charlie was sunburned and had a patch of poison oak on his wrist. He asked Jim to take him home rather than camp out for the night, and when Jim dismissed this suggestion, Charlie whined like a toddler. He said he wished he was back home with his mother and Kevin, didn't understand why he had to be on this vacation with his father rather than playing video games on Kevin's entertainment center. Jim became very angry. He threw a shoe into the ground so it bounced like a ball, and cursed through his lips.

Then he calmed down a bit and told Charlie to go rinse off his feet and entertain himself by the creek while he prepared the fire to roast their hotdogs and fashioned a clothing line for their swim trunks.

When it was time to go to bed, Charlie once again begged his father to take him home, claiming that he was afraid of the dark. He told Jim that, at home, he slept with the overhead light on. He said he hadn't wanted to confess earlier, because he didn't want his father to think him a coward, but the dark did something to him, he explained. Monsters in his head.

Jim had quickly pulled out both flashlights and propped them up in the corners of the tent so that it was very light inside. "No more dark," he said to Charlie. "Capiche?"

Charlie shook his head and pointed his thumb in the direction of the tent opening. "I know it's still *out there*," he said.

"What?" His father said, with exasperation. "What now, Charlie? And out *where*?"

Charlie said, "It's *dark* out there."

Jim became angry once again, certain that Charlie was not in fact afraid of the dark but simply inventing an excuse to go home early, even as Charlie continued to insist that this wasn't the case.

"I don't believe you," Jim said. "I hear what you're saying, and I don't believe you're telling me the truth."

Charlie was inconsolable.

Furiously, Jim collapsed their tent, packed their things, and drove Charlie home.

Laura married Kevin the following summer, when Charlie was seven.

Laura didn't like how much Jim was drinking, and she took that up with the court. Weekends with Charlie became Friday nights only, then just a few hours on a Sunday afternoon. Their time together was so short and so weird that Jim often felt even more disconnected from his son after a visit than he had before. It killed him to hear Charlie talk about his new home at Kevin's; all the things he did there, all the things he had. Kevin could give Charlie anything, it seemed.

Jim eventually lost his job at Kia. He wasn't sleeping, and seldom made it in by nine o'clock, when technically his shift started at eight. Not like it mattered that much, anyway, he thought. He was no good at sales, so they had already demoted him to inventory and maintenance. Twice, they caught him drinking. They gave him warnings; HR knew he was going through some tough times and they extended an extra measure of compassion, but he pushed them too far. Still, they all agreed that Jim was not a *bad guy*, and they wished him well. They offered him a good reference, and helped out with his paperwork so he was able to collect unemployment for a few months. Like clockwork, Jim took his unemployment money to the liquor store and then to the Seneca Casino on the very day he received it. He'd spend it all by midnight. He couldn't remember what it felt like to wake in the morning without a crippling hangover. The grace period for unemployment ran out, and he was looking at bankruptcy. He started filling out applications for everything from plumbing to a Subway sandwich artist.

A buddy got Jim a job in maintenance for Decker Quality Foods, out of nearby Dunkirk, New York. He did this for a few years before they transferred him to Butte, Montana, where they were opening a new plant. Jim left willingly, signing a one-year contract. It was more money, and he barely saw Charlie anyway. He needed a change of scene.

Jim drummed his fingers briskly on the bar in this new town, this *new scene*. "I try not to think on it too much," he said to the stranger. "That's where this comes in." He tapped his finger on his whiskey glass. "Can't sleep without turning it all off, then I wake up thirsty for the next one."

The guy sipped his coffee and went back to his steak. He was hacking at the thing like it was a leather jacket.

"How is it?" Jim said.

"Steak's shit," the guy said, "But the potatoes aren't half bad."

"How long you been sober?" Jim said, and he added, "If you don't mind."

"Not long enough."

"It gets easier, does it?" Jim said. "You quit waking up thirsty for the next one?"

"Nah," said the guy. He set down his silverware, wiped his face, and sipped his coffee. "You never quit being thirsty for it, you just get used to the thirst."

"*Well*," Jim said. "That's a sad state of affairs." He dug a thumbnail into a knot on the wooden bar. Scratched at its black center. "Pickin' up out there," Jim added, nodding toward the window behind the bar, where raindrops exploded against the glass.

Reminded of his divorce, Jim's thoughts now turned to the woman responsible for it. In the moment when they met, the feeling of an unfamiliar hand on his leg seemed like the most impressive thing that had happened to him in years. The Bills game was on the bar television, and she'd said her granddad used to play in the NFL. Jim had never heard of the guy, but he was impressed with her knowledge of the team. Her eyes were the color of black coffee. There was something soft and vulnerable but also brave and dangerous about how easily, how quickly and carelessly, she revealed herself. Like she hadn't been taught to do otherwise, like she didn't know that the world was mean. Or maybe she'd just come to terms with it. She didn't seem upset when Jim had called to inform her that Laura had found out and that he wouldn't be calling again. She didn't seem very surprised. Her TV was on in the background.

Jim swallowed some whiskey. He was very drunk now. He'd have to walk home in the rain, leave his car in the company lot. Might as well have one more. He polished off the small, slippery pills of ice remaining in his glass and the last of the watered-down whiskey.

"Whattya reckon's worse . . ." Jim said, turning to face the guy. "Telling a lie, or not believing a truth?"

The guy didn't respond right away. He emptied another creamer into his coffee.

"I'm guilty of both, of course," Jim offered quickly.

"Suppose . . ." the guy finally spoke but then paused for another moment, a forkful of steak suspended in midair, near his lips. "Suppose that depends on who you're lying to, and what you're choosing not to believe."

"There you are," Jim said. He didn't dislike that answer, but he felt intensely empty and pessimistic.

"You know what I'd give just about anything for?" Jim said.

"Hm?" The guy speared another large bite of steak, dipped it in ketchup, lifted it to his mouth. Rain struck the window behind the bar in a gusty burst.

Jim tapped his empty glass when the bartender passed, indicating that he'd like another. "I'd give just about *any*thing to wake up one day into a whole different life," he said.

The guy chewed his steak, deposited a fatty bit into his napkin, and swallowed. "Then I guess you gotta die, brother."

CASH FOR GOLD

Marty had an oily brown bag full of donuts from the truck that sat outside the IGA on Saturday mornings, and a tall black coffee from his friend Randall Bear's EZ Mart. It was very cold outside, and very warm in his sunny car. He was heading north.

Ten days earlier, Marty had received the awaited phone call from his doctor. Marty was sitting in his La-Z-Boy when he took this call, and he could tell from the tone of his doctor's voice that he'd better sit back and make himself as comfortable as possible for the news that was to come. He yanked on the wooden handle at his right side to elevate the footrest of his chair, and reclined back. Staring upward, Marty watched a stinkbug as it traveled very slowly in the direction of the ceiling light fixture. He kicked his slippers off his feet.

The cancer had spread, Dr. Vann announced. The growth in his stomach was now the size of a fist, and there were new spots on Marty's liver. None of the attempted treatments had slowed the spread of the cancer, and they had run out of options, even experimental ones. Dr. Vann carefully explained that his recommendation, therefore, was to forego further treatments, so that Marty could live out his remaining months free of the discomfort, inconvenience, and side effects of the chemo. "So you can be free," Dr. Vann said, using this word a second time.

Marty felt almost nothing at this, except for his own exhale. The slow and peaceful emptying of his lungs. The sweet numbness that does not accompany denial so much as the confirmation of a long-held suspicion. Marty realized in this moment how ready he was for this news; how perfectly *prepared* for this knowledge, as though he'd just opened the front door of his house to a guest whose company he didn't particularly enjoy, but whose visit was long overdue.

Marty agreed that he too thought it best to discontinue his treatments, and Dr. Vann expressed his relief at this decision.

Marty hung up the phone and stared at the ceiling above him as it pulsed and rippled with patterns like the surface of water, as though he and everything else in the room was underwater, swaying in neat rhythms, releasing bubbles in slow motion. The stinkbug lifted its legs one at a time but didn't seem to be heading in any particular direction.

As Marty allowed this strange, new truth to settle into his old bones, he started to formulate thoughts. But these thoughts were not about the cancer in his stomach or in his blood; how it had gotten there and why it couldn't be contained. He didn't think about the time and money spent on worthless treatments, or the possibility that one of those homeopathic methods Randall's wife Denise Bear was always emailing about could have been more successful. He didn't think about a funeral or how he would go about delivering this news to Randall.

What he thought about was the Mouse in her tiny yellow swimsuit on that first day at the beach when she bounded out into the big lake, unable to swim, hollering and splashing out under that white sun, oblivious to the dangers of this earth. He wondered if, in the many years since that summer, anyone had taught her how to swim, or if to this day she remained a starfish.

Poor Tracy. *Poor Tracy.* Tears suddenly heated Marty's cheeks and he rocked himself painfully in his La-Z-Boy. His heart ached for her, both in sorrow and sympathy, and also, suddenly, intensely, for her company. Poor Tracy had never chosen to be a starfish. Not any more, Marty reckoned, than Tracy's mother had ever chosen to be whatever she was, nor Marty, whatever he was.

Later that same night, Marty started to pack up his house with a fresh, purposeful energy. He organized some bags for the dump, some bags for the thrift store, some stuff to offer to Randall before junking it. He flushed his medications down the toilet. He bought a plane ticket to Buffalo, booked a room at the Budget Inn. He considered where he might take Tracy fishing, if that would interest her, if she was able to get any time off work, and what they'd likely catch in Lake Erie at this time of year. He watched an episode of *Monsters and Mysteries of Alaska* on the National Geographic Channel. He busied himself until practically midnight, and that night he slept very soundly, even through the violent clunking of walnuts as they fell to his roof from their skinny black limbs.

Today, he was heading north in order to do his business at the cash-for-gold place in Arcadia before flying down to Buffalo. He had all his fishing lures with him and aimed to remove the gold and gemstones he'd carefully woven into each piece, in order to exchange them for cash. It was something he'd done for years, hand-crafting these little lures and jigs using trinkets he dug up on the beach. It was an odd hobby, he knew, especially for someone who didn't even do all that much fishing anymore, but it was something to do. Something to make.

He wasn't sure how many of the pieces in question actually contained real gold, but that's what he aimed to find out, and hoped he'd get a nice chunk of change that he could offer to Tracy. In the past, when he'd sent her jewelry, she'd always been so concerned with whether or not it was real gold, and he'd never bothered to check. Now, he figured, he had the time; he'd go ahead and find out for her. He'd made an appointment with one of those cash-for-gold jewelers who was willing to give a quick look at every single piece. For the ones that were worth something, Marty would remove them from the lure and exchange them for money on the spot, so it was all sorted out for Tracy.

His flight was at 8:00 a.m. tomorrow. He had rented out a room in the Budget Inn in Tonawanda for a whole week, with the option of a monthly rate if he decided to stick around. He'd cleared the dates with Tracy, but hadn't told her of his intention to stay for more than a few days. He'd wait and feel things out on that.

Just this morning, at the EZ Mart, Randall Bear had said, "You *kiddin'*? You're really gonna tear apart all them lures you worked so hard on, just to have a little cash to give her? And you're going all the way to Arcadia, that long drive by yourself? Then a flight down to Buffalo in two weeks? A *one-way* ticket?!" Randall shook his head. "*You're* the one's sick. *She* oughtta come up here to see *you*."

Marty said, "If my kid doesn't want to come up here to see me, then that's my fault, not hers, bud."

He knew Randall was just trying to look out for him. And he knew it probably wasn't wise to be driving himself around like this, but now that he was off the treatments, he felt as good as new, even though they had told him that everything inside was going positively haywire. He had felt better these past ten days than he had in a very long time. Loads of energy, thinking positively. He wasn't sure if it was the absence of chemo in his system or what, but he felt downright *good*. Strong, sturdy, clear-headed. Funny that way, cancer. How little you could actually know about the body you'd lived in for your whole damn life, how wrong you could be about your own insides.

Marty pulled a donut from the bag and bit into it. Granulated sugar flew into his nostrils. The cake was hot and doughy in the center. The last radio station he'd been listening to had gone to static, so he just turned it off altogether. It really was a beautiful morning. Soon, he would pass the white beaches of Sleeping Bear Dunes. He blinked slowly, pleasantly, like a sleepy cat, happy in the sunshine.

Out to Marty's left, a gunmetal-gray Lake Michigan tumbled over and over and over itself, and Marty thought back to that day on the beach several weeks earlier, the day on which he had encountered that strange woman on the beach.

Marty was out with his metal detector on that day.

It was a cold and gusty one, with fat, low clouds the color of wet cement.

A fit of nausea interrupted Marty's search, and he made his way up to a part of the dune that was protected from wind. He removed his bag to use it as a pillow and closed his eyes to settle his roiling stomach.

Marty woke to the sudden, chilly awareness of a large presence in front of him. He flinched instinctively, knees buckling up toward his chest. He stared up at the figure, colorful shapes dancing in front of his eyes while they focused.

It was a woman's face on a broad, manly frame, staring down at him. She didn't move or speak. Marty scrambled backward and to his feet. The sand was shifty beneath him, and for a moment he dipped around on legs that felt weak and helpless and too skinny beneath him. He used his detector as a cane to steady himself.

The woman was several inches taller than Marty and her shoulders were twice as wide. She wore a man's hat, a neoprene vest, a flannel shirt. Her face was dark and beautiful and rough, like she'd been carved with a tool that was very sharp, but a bit too large. Marty guessed she was from the Chippewa reservation ten miles north of Manistee. It's where Marty got his gas and cigarettes and locked his car when he went in to pay. He'd only use the shitter in there for an absolute emergency. It was a one-stall unit around the outside of the station, and to get in you had to ask the cashier for a key strung through a hole in a piece of driftwood.

The woman's baseball cap was pale yellow with white netting, and beneath it her hair was long and straight and black, reaching all the way to her elbows with some streaks of gray. Her cheekbones were smooth and high, the color of a clay planter.

"You're not dead," the woman said. She barely moved her lips when she spoke, not even enough for him to see her teeth.

"No, I ain't," Marty said. He was gripping his detector like a weapon.

"Just checking," the woman said. It could have been a joke, Marty thought, but she didn't deliver it that way.

The woman turned to walk away, down toward the water. She wore brown boots that went halfway up her calves, where her jeans were tucked into them. She moved like she was very strong, but tired.

"What the—" Marty said. "Who *are* you?" he called after her.

She said something over her shoulder and continued to walk away.

"Say again?" Marty shouted into a faceful of wind.

The woman turned around only long enough to say, "Cook," then she continued on her way, toward the water.

Marty set his detector on the ground in order to follow her. She moved with such large strides that he had to jog to catch up.

"Hey!" Marty called, moving faster now than he had in months, skipping down the dune and kicking up clouds of sand. "Hey! Listen to me!"

When she didn't turn and in fact her pace seemed to quicken, Marty felt something powerfully helpless and panicky shoot through him. Catching up to her suddenly mattered a great deal to him, and he didn't know if he'd be able. He ran faster, nearly losing his balance as the sand swallowed his feet.

He ran faster and waved his arms.

"Hey!" he screamed after her. "Why don't you slow down here?"

What would make her stop?

"Hey!" he screamed, "*I'm dying*, for Christ's sakes, how am I supposed to keep up? Hey! I said I'm *dying*!"

Cook finally stopped. She looked out into the water for a time, then turned to face Marty when he reached her. Marty gasped for air. His whole middle screamed in defiance of every move, every breath. He grasped his stomach, wheezed, and sat down on the sand.

Cook lowered herself to sit next to him.

"I said, I'm dying," Marty repeated.

Cook looked at him as though this information was not entirely sad, nor surprising.

"I'm dying," Marty said again, still gasping. "I'm waiting for a call from my doc, and I'll find out in a week or two how long I've got, but I know it's not going to be long. I know I'm dying. Do you hear me?" He felt desperate, finished, *wrecked*. "Do you hear me, lady?" He coughed and pounded the sand with his knuckles. "I'm *dying*," he said, "And . . . and it's not what I wanted."

"How's that?" Cook asked.

"I just thought . . ." Marty's voice had cracked into many pitches and he felt his sand-covered hands go to his cheeks in a gesture of despair. "I just always thought that you'd get to end up with the people you wanna end up with. You know, the people who meant something. The ones you *belong* with."

Marty's chest heaved. Something crushing, very deep inside. Deeper than the cancer. "You know, like your mom. Your pop. Friends from way back, the ones who already kicked the bucket, and the ones who are still around. And even, *especially*, the people you fall out with. Ex-wives. Kids. *My kid.*" Marty's voice broke again, lurching out in high and odd tones. "I thought you got to still *belong* with these people."

Marty looked out toward the water. Angry little whitecaps made their way up the shore and broke into frothy fingers.

Tears dropped from Marty's chin.

"You know," he continued, "I never believed in Heaven or any of that mumbo jumbo, but I still thought . . . Well, I guess I didn't think it would end up just me alone in a room with a tube stickin' out my butt. I just thought there'd be a place where we'd all sit down together, all these people who matter, that we'd all enjoy a stiff drink and a good laugh." Marty wiped his eyes. "That we could always *belong* together."

He looked at Cook. She wore a calm, easy expression, almost like she was holding in a smile.

"Where am I gonna go, anyway?" Marty said, not certain why he was demanding this information from Cook, but it was the questions he'd longed to ask someone, anyone, for some time. And he was split open now, anyway, unafraid of the answers she might offer. "Whattya reckon it's like?"

"What, death?"

Marty nodded.

"Could be . . ." Cook paused. "Could be that it's just another place." She made a soft gesture out toward the water. "Just another place you've never been."

Marty considered this. "Do you know something? I've never been south of the Southtowns, never in my whole life," he said. "Ain't that something?" He lifted a handful of sand and allowed the grains to slide through his fingers like silk ribbons.

Cook rose to her feet and dusted off her large hands. Then she turned and headed north, along the shore.

Marty thought of following her, but he was exhausted, and could see that her strides were now impossibly large. A sudden gust of wind rushed across the beach and seized Marty's lungs with its chill. He watched as her form dissolved into the landscape and he felt a sweet, balmy nothingness, like he was on the brink of something too big and too strange to fear.

Now, these words returned to Marty as he soared up Route 6 in his little white Dodge Omni, past the ice cream place with the air dancer vanilla cone rising and falling and flailing out toward him. *Another place I've never been* . . . there were so, so many of those!

He passed three identical blue for-rent cabins with signs out front identifying them as Wynken, Blynken, and Nod. He passed a Mobil station with yellow plastic bags over the pumps and two-by-fours over the front door and windows. He reached for another donut. He had twenty miles to go before he reached Arcadia.

Marty passed the Quinn Family Diner with a handful of pickup trucks in the lot. The woods to his right became thicker, and the area more remote—he went a few miles without passing any buildings at all. The leaves were at their most brilliant, every shade of gold you could imagine, and spinning loosely from their branches in the sunlight. It had rained the night before, and a thick, wet leaf flopped onto Marty's windshield like a hand and didn't move.

Oddly enough, the bright sun in his eyes made him sleepier. He reached into his center console for his sunglasses, but they weren't there.

Marty reached the top of a nice, round, Michigan hill, and before him the road sailed downward into a wild grove of eastern white pines before veering to the right. Out his window to the left, Marty could still see the lake sparkling with saw-toothed whitecaps. He yawned. Maybe he'd go fishing off the channel tonight, if he got back at a reasonable hour. It would all depend how much time this cash-for-gold business took. He wanted to get to bed early this evening so he'd be in good shape for his flight tomorrow morning. He was already packed.

He wiped sugar from his lips. He felt so sleepy. He tried to think which bait would be best for those Lake Erie perch he'd been reading about. Years ago, he'd had pretty good success with a bugeye jig, but he wasn't sure if this was the right season for that. A furry worm might be better.

Marty blinked slowly. The sun was so warm on his face. He blinked again, slower still. Life felt unbelievably uncomplicated. And then, for one long, lovely moment just before he nodded his chin softly to his chest in sleep, Marty completely forgot everything. Forgot that his foot depressed a pedal and his fingers clutched a wheel, forgot where he was going, forgot that a sky was a sky, and that he was a man. Forgot everything except for the things in his heart, the things that were there all along, the things that required nothing of him and couldn't be forgotten because they were as real and as much a part of him as his bones, his blood.

CITRINE

Tracy's invite arrived a full month ahead of Thanksgiving. Underneath the details, her cousin Shelly had signed for Mac and the kids and sketched a cornucopia in orange glitter pen. Tracy stuck the Thanksgiving invite to her refrigerator with a Papa John's magnet. Several days later, Shelly called to follow up.

"What's your excuse this year?" she said.

"I might have to work."

"*Hah*! Got you. The restaurant's closed on Thanksgiving. I knew you would say that so I called and checked."

"Oh, for Pete's sake, Shelly. Well look, I didn't want to say so, but I might be spending it with my boyfriend's family."

"Who's your boyfriend? Why don't you bring him to ours? We haven't had you at a family thing in ages and my kids barely know you from Adam."

Tracy stared at the invite and picked at the glitter with her fingernail. "I'll let you know by next weekend."

Tracy was waiting to see if Greenie would invite her to his family Thanksgiving. She'd never met the Greens, even though they lived in her neighborhood, and Greenie had been spending a night or two a week at Tracy's place for many months now.

Later that week, Tracy went to Jo-Ann Fabric on her way in to the restaurant. She picked up a baggie of hypoallergenic earring hooks, a hot glue gun, and a twelve-pack of the translucent, cigarette-sized glue sticks. She'd come up with the idea for this project while sorting through her father's ramshackle little home up in Michigan several weeks earlier.

It was the first time she'd set foot in the place since she was ten years old, but when her father died, all of the administrative stuff fell on her. There was nobody else, the funeral director informed her. *You're it.* So she'd driven nine hours each way to empty the place. She'd hauled almost everything off to the local Goodwill, except for his metal detector, which she disassembled in order to pack it neatly back into the original box, and several shoe boxes full of her father's signature fishing lures. Later in life, he'd gotten into custom-designing his own lures, weaving some junky little metal trinket into the feathery bit. Tracy remembered that he had once taught her how certain fish are attracted to a bit of sparkle in addition to the bait itself, but she could no longer remember which. He had decorated each lure with a little gold charm or ring, a coin, a few chain links, a broken-off necklace clasp. He had all sorts of knickknacks to choose from after years of metal detecting. When Tracy was sifting through these materials, she took care to hang onto all these nice feathery ones that hadn't faded or been gnawed on, because she thought they'd make nice earrings.

Tracy told the cashier at Jo-Ann Fabric her plan for the supplies. She had brought one of the fishing lures in, and the cashier complimented Tracy's father's handiwork. She recommended that Tracy get some extra thread, to wind around the base of each earring so the glue wouldn't show.

Tracy said, "I think I'll manage."

When she got into work, she told Greenie about the supplies in her car. He was on a stepladder behind the bar with a clipboard clamped in his armpit. He glanced down over his shoulder and said, "You sure there's nothin' valuable in that stuff? You could probably get a little cash for some of the gold or stones, if any of it's real."

"Doubt it," she said. She was so sure of this that she hadn't even bothered to check. The last few times her father had sent gifts, she'd inquired about the number of karats, and he didn't even know if the damn things were real gold. She couldn't imagine that there was anything worthwhile in the mess of lures.

Greenie said, "Are you gonna give them out to your family at the holidays?"

"We don't really do presents with extended family. I was thinking of selling them—you know I've been talking jewelry business for a while. Speaking of family, what's going on with Thanksgiving?"

"My folks are hosting this year," Greenie said, "My sister's gonna be home from school. What about you?"

Tracy fingered the collar of her silk shirt. It was big on her; the shoulder seams fell nearly to her elbows, but when she paired it with her black skirt and leopard print belt it was very flattering and she always got compliments.

"I was going to see if you wanted to come to my cousin Shelly's," she said. "She lives in Rochester. They're all right. We could do both families if you wanted, mine in the afternoon, then back to your folks' place for the evening . . . Or we could just do one or the other, or . . ."

Greenie got down from the stepladder and sipped his power-ade. His upper lip was stained cherry red. He looked like a doll. "You really think we should start doing family stuff together?"

Tracy scowled into her lap. They had to keep their relationship quiet around the workplace on account of being coworkers, but she wasn't clear on why things had to be so hush-hush with friends and family outside of the restaurant too.

She got up to straighten the stack of high chairs and booster seats by her host stand.

"Not trying to be a jerk," Greenie said when she returned, "but I'm telling you, the age thing is really gonna throw my folks. I'm just trying to ease them into it."

"Fine by me," Tracy said. She lined up fifteen little white dishes across the bar and opened a fresh box of the individually packaged creamers that didn't require refrigeration. She put a handful of creamers in each dish. "But you say it like it's such a thing. We're not that far apart and it's not like we *look* weird together."

Greenie finished his PowerAde and tossed the empty bottle underhand into the garbage can. He punched some numbers into the calculator at his register. "I'll think it over, Trace. Do you have to know now? I'll think it over and let you know soon."

The restaurant was decorated for autumn, with burnt-orange tapestries hung across the far wall, burgundy candles and an ear of Indian corn on each table. A dried sunflower lay across each windowsill, next to the little potted jade plants. At the beginning of every shift, Tracy fixed Greenie's arrangement at the bar, since he didn't have an eye for detail, like she did.

Greenie grabbed a gourd from his arrangement and rolled it down the bar toward Tracy.

"This thing smell right to you?"

The gourd veered to the left and dropped onto one of the barstools. Tracy retrieved the gourd and sniffed it.

She shrugged. "It doesn't smell *wrong*," she said, passing it back and forth between her hands.

Tracy's cousin Tom was smoking a cigarette on Shelly's porch when Tracy arrived. His glass of red was full nearly to the brim, and several crusted drip stains lined the outside. The stem of the glass had an orange pipe cleaner wound tightly around it, and a green construction-paper leaf was scotch-taped to the base.

"Hi, T," Tom said. He held his cigarette at his lips with his index finger and thumb, the rest of his fingers curled over and around it in a loose fist, like he was trying to protect it from the cold. His forehead opened up to bare pink scalp that was dented once, deep and straight right across the crown. The hair that remained around his ears was dark and wiry. He wore stylish glasses with tortoiseshell frames and had an enterprising little moustache.

Tracy brushed a crumb from his chest.

"How you holding up?" he said.

"How do you mean?"

"Your dad. I haven't talked to you since." Tom said. "I guess it's good it happened the way it did, huh? You were saying he only had a few months anyway?"

"Yeah, that's true." Tracy reached into her purse, pulled out a Kleenex and wiped the snow off her boots. "I'm doing fine. A-OK."

"Not to be morbid, Trace, but with cancer on both sides, you should really get checked. You get those screenings and stuff?"

"Sure, I do."

"Glad you're doing OK. So, where's your date? Shelly said you RSVP'd two."

"He's with his family. He begged me to come to theirs, but Shelly really wanted me here. I'm gonna duck out of this thing a little early to spend the evening with him."

"Well thank goodness you're here now, for my sake. I thought I'd be the only one flying solo." Tom ran his hand across the porch railing to gather some snow, and packed a snowball with both hands. He wound up and threw it like a baseball toward Tracy's truck. It smacked into the passenger's wheel.

Tracy aimed her key at her truck to lock it. The truck beeped twice and the headlights flashed.

"You think I need my emergency brake?"

"Nah."

Shelly greeted Tracy just inside the door. She had lost weight and her lipstick matched her shirt. She wiped her hands on her white mini-apron and they hugged.

"I'm glad you came early," Shelly said. "They're calling for a foot this afternoon, I was worried you'd run into that on your way."

"My truck is great in this stuff."

"I don't know where the kids are," Shelly said. She hollered their names then turned back to Tracy. "You won't even recognize Jay, he's grown a foot in the past month. Kristen wears glasses now. Make yourself at home. Oh—do you mind?" Shelly nodded toward a neat lineup of shoes to the left of the entrance. Tracy had to sit down on an antique wooden chair next to the door in order to pull off her zippered black boots. Shelly disappeared into the kitchen.

"This-a-way," Tom said. "I'll get you a drink, then introduce you to Mac's lame friends and we can go goochy-goochy goo at their babies."

Shelly and Mac had added an entire wing to their downstairs since Tracy had last been there. The dining arrangement was an impressive lineup of card tables connected with light blue tablecloths, and it stretched from the far end of the living room the entire way through the downstairs, ending in the winterized patio. It was a nice house, there was no getting around that. It wasn't all that much bigger than Tracy's home, but it was new and immaculate, with beige carpet and leather couches and a huge framed cityscape photo of Buffalo at night. They already had their Christmas tree, a real spruce, decorated with red tinsel and Santa's made from felt.

Tom introduced Tracy to Mac's brother and his wife, then Shelly's best friend and her family, and a handsome couple who didn't speak much English, from Shelly and Mac's church.

"Helen and Johann are Germans," Shelly said, joining the conversation over Tracy's shoulder, "visiting all the way from Chad. They do mission work there."

Tracy had two more glasses of wine. She greeted all the family members whose names she remembered. The ones who knew about her father offered condolences. She got a lot of compliments on her outfit. She'd sewn her skirt herself, and explained to everyone who commented on it that she was doing a whole collection of clothing and jewelry. She asked how much they would be willing to spend on a skirt like this. It was knee-length, black chiffon with vertical stripes of citrine, and it was secured at her waist with a gold seashell button. She'd read in a fashion magazine that citrine was *the color* to wear this fall, and she had picked out the pattern and material with Greenie's family in mind.

In the kitchen, Shelly put her to work on the veggie plate. Tracy dumped a bag of baby carrots and a jar of olives onto different compartments of the glass serving tray. She sliced up red peppers and celery hearts and cucumber disks. Next to her, Shelly opened the oven and plunged a meat thermometer into the turkey. Dried zinnia heads were lined up across the island counter, and Tom was rearranging them when Shelly's children came into the kitchen.

"You guys remember your Aunt Tracy?" Tom said.

Kristen was wearing a sombrero, a navy velvet dress and ballet slippers. Her teeth were tiny and rounded with spaces between them, like loosely strung pearls. Jay wore pleather chaps over his khaki pants and he had a plastic bow and arrow, which he aimed at Tracy's face, but didn't shoot. Shelly ushered the kids off to their rooms to get decent before the meal.

"Nice kids," Tracy said.

"Speaking of kids," Tom said, "is your boyfriend that bartender you introduced me to a while back? You still robbin' that cradle?" He elbowed her.

"Greenie's not that much younger. It's not like we *look* weird together. You're drunk, aren't you? And yes, he's my boyfriend, but it's not even that serious."

"All right, crabby," said Tom.

They went to the dining room, where Tom pulled two chairs out from the table and sat down next to her. Tracy ate a handful of candy corn from a little porcelain dish that sat in the center of the table, next to rooster-shaped salt and pepper shakers. Directly across the table was a woman whose face looked like it had been boiled. She picked at a hard crumb on her fork, her hands horned and powdery. She introduced herself as Mac's aunt, and Tracy had to tell her three times that Tom was her cousin, not her husband.

Once everyone was seated, Shelly stood and clinked her glass with her spoon. "Let's send the wine around," she said. "Make sure all the adults have a full glass before we say grace." Mac sent two half-empty bottles of Merlot around the long table and opened a fresh Chardonnay. He closed his eyes and smelled the cork before passing the bottle to his left.

Tracy raised her hand. "I have something, Shelly," she said. "I have something quick before the prayer."

Tracy reached underneath her chair and pulled out a shoe box. It was royal blue and had the Adidas logo on every side.

Tracy pushed her place setting forward to make room for the box on the table. She ran her index finger beneath the masking tape she'd put on all four sides of the lid to secure it.

"My dad loved the lake," Tracy said loudly to the whole room. She opened the box and pulled out one bright purple feather earring attached to a tiny tarnished gold coin with a hole drilled through the center. "He took me fishing when I was little. He's gone now but I saved some of his leftover fishing lures, which he decorated with some other little trinkets he found on the beach. I used his materials to make these earrings. I've wanted to get into the jewelry-making business for a while."

Tracy lifted the earring and swung it in a slow semicircle in front of her, then handed it to Tom. "You can pass it around," she said.

Tom examined the earring up close and squeezed at the pea-sized glue bubble a little bit.

"If anyone wants a pair, you can talk to me after the meal," Tracy said.

Shelly retrieved her napkin from her lap and ran it over her lips. "What a darling idea, Trace. Marty sure did love to fish, didn't he?"

Tracy stirred her ice water with her knife. She watched one of Shelly's friends down the table wrinkle her nose distastefully at the earring when it reached her.

"I remember," Shelly continued brightly, "how Marty used to take the three of us fishing when he'd come down for a visit, Tracy and me and Tom here too. Marty always baited my hook for me because I didn't like that part. We fished off the canal, in the Niagara River, and sometimes off that, what was it called? Oh, the Nowak pier just upriver. Oh, and sometimes he'd take us out on the big lake in his little boat. That was such a treat."

Tracy stared at her cousin. She could hear the blood rushing into her face while Shelly gazed up at the ceiling fan. Shelly's freshly highlighted hair fell back from her face, exposing dangly green earrings that matched her necklace. Shelly looked, as usual, like she was a woman who really knew how the world worked. "Let's all raise our glasses to Marty," Shelly said.

Around the table, people said, "Marty," and they looked sideways at Tracy, and they drank.

The earring had made it around the table. Tom handed it to Tracy and she dropped it into the shoe box, then tucked the box under her elbow while lifting the legs of her chair to back it soundlessly away from the table.

"'Scusing myself," she whispered to Tom, while Mac started to pray.

In the kitchen, Tracy yanked a frosty bottle of vodka from the freezer and poured herself a glass. There was plenty of food still out on the stove and countertop, but she reached instead into the pocket of her skirt for the warm string cheese she'd forgotten about on the drive down. A *Cooking Light* magazine was clothespinned open to a sweet potato recipe. Tracy removed the clothespin and held it between her teeth while she paged through the magazine. She eased herself onto the counter so her legs dangled, heels knocking against the cupboard, and started into an article on the best and worst uses for Splenda.

Mac and Shelly's little black Scottish Terrier trotted in, stood at Tracy's feet, and rubbed its chin against her ankle bone. "Go away, Lucas," she said. The vodka was cold and syrupy on the roof of her mouth. She tried to ignore the Thanksgiving toasts still going on in the other room.

Shelly appeared at the doorway a few minutes later. "What's wrong, Trace?"

Tracy slapped the magazine shut and looked up. "What would you guess?"

Shelly blinked. "All I know is that we're all out there having a good time, and you're in here drinking vodka and muttering under your breath and eating—is that a string cheese? Did you bring that?"

Tracy set her glass down hard on the counter. "You didn't have to go and make like you have all these nice memories of fishing with my dad in his boat out on the lake. You know he never took you out there. When he fished with you, it was always just off the pier or at the shore. His boat wouldn't seat more than just me and him."

"You've got to be kidding me." Shelly's face stretched long and open. "He took us out there on the lake at least half a dozen times. I swear on my kids. I remember it clear as day. It was tight, but the boat wasn't too small. All four of us could go out at once."

"That's a load of crap, Shelly." Tracy slid off the counter. "You were along on the trips to the canal. And to the river, maybe. But you never came out on the lake with us. That was the best fishing, where we got the walleye, but he'd never take anyone other than me because there wasn't room in his boat."

Shelly looked stunned. "See this is what's wrong with this family," she said. Lucas was at her feet, so she picked him up around his ribs, carried him to the basement door, and dropped him from so high that he squeaked softly. "Here I am, trying to tell a nice memory . . ."

Tom rounded the corner into the kitchen.

Tracy turned to him. "Do you remember these fishing trips with my dad that Shelly's going on about? These ones in the boat, *out on the lake*?"

"Marty was all right," Tom said. "I don't remember that he ever took me out in his boat, but my memory's for shit."

Tracy looked back at Shelly, who threw both of her hands out in front of her. "I swear to you, Tracy. Why would I make something like that up?" she said. "I don't care enough to make something like that up!"

Tracy crumpled up the string cheese wrapper in her hand and went to the kitchen sink. "Because you're a one-upper," she said over her shoulder.

Shelly had always had a nervous habit of clenching her fists when she was upset, working them in and out while she searched for the right word, careful to never fully lose control. Tracy didn't turn around, but Shelly was quiet for a moment, and Tracy imagined that she had both hands pumping now like she was giving blood. She heard Shelly whisper something sharp to Tom, then something about her guests, then she left the kitchen.

Tracy sipped her vodka. There were morsels of food cemented to the base of the sink, and a stalk of celery coming up through the garbage disposal. A fake candle with a bulb for a flame was perched on the windowsill above the sink and it shone bright and golden. It even had fake drips of wax.

Tom joined Tracy at the window. Outside, a greasy-looking crow was picking at seeds from a bird feeder that hung on a wire from a young, thin maple tree. Tracy could see across Shelly's and Mac's lawn all the way into the kitchen of the next house over, where bodies moved back and forth across the window in pairs, swaying and bending to laugh.

"Don't let her get you all wound up," Tom said. "Who cares if she went out on the boat with you or if she didn't? What's the point of going back and forth over memories anyway? It's like . . . poking dead roadkill with a stick."

The house smelled like so many good things that Tracy's entire body felt wobbly. She listened to Lucas whining at the basement door. She retrieved a turkey scrap from the compost and cracked the door to deliver it to him. She finished her vodka in one swallow and her sinuses burned.

Tracy straightened her watch over her wrist. "I'm outta here. Greenie's expecting me soon anyway."

The snow was wet. Tracy held the shoe box over her head to protect her hair on her way out to her truck. She had a specific pair in mind for Greenie's sister, who was wearing neon greens in most of the family pictures Tracy had seen.

She got into her truck and turned the heat on high. She ran the wipers to clear away the inch of feathery snow that had collected on the windshield. The wipers squeaked. Her book on tape started back up, and she paused it. She dialed Greenie.

"Happy Thanksgiving," she said.

"Your voice sounds weird."

"I'm all fired up. I fought with my cousin. The one I told you about." Tracy shivered and adjusted her vents. "I'll be on my way to your folks' place in five, just need to stop for gas and a coffee. Remind me again what's the address?"

"You sure you're OK to drive?" Greenie said.

"I'll be fine."

"It's really coming down."

"Greenie, I'm fine," she said. "I've got my chains put on."

Tracy heard the soft chafe of Greenie's palm over his mouthpiece, and his muffled voice when he called, "*Nobody, Ma*," then something else that she couldn't make out. His voice came back strong. "Trace, I think you should just spend today there with your family. We can talk tomorrow."

Tracy didn't want to cry but it was all gathered right behind her face and it was hot and urgent. It came out in a single, heavy sob, and then she was done. She hung up her phone and threw it onto the floor mat of the passenger seat, where it thunked against the bottle of red she'd picked up to take to the Greens'.

How was it that she hadn't once in her entire life cried about her very own father, *not once*; not on the day he left, not over the visits he missed, not when he was diagnosed, or the day he died. Not one single tear for her very own father. Yet Greenie, that child, that selfish, stupid boy, he could straight-up squash her in half a second. How many times she had tentatively rehearsed this day in her mind.

Tracy lit a cigarette.

She woke to tapping at her cheek. She sat up and rubbed the left side of her face, which was icy cold from being pressed against the window of her truck. There was a spot of fog on her window. She rubbed it away with the inside of her wrist. It was dark out. The German from Chad was at her window.

She felt around and beneath herself but couldn't locate her keys to roll down the window, so she opened her door. She was met by a screaming wintry gust that took her breath away.

"I'm sorry." The man propped his arms on her door and the roof of her truck so that she was protected from the wind. "You're in our path." His face was pearl-colored in the moonlight and it was lovely, made up of flat, even planes and perfect angles, like origami. He pointed at the car parked in front of Tracy, where she could see the back of his wife's head in the passenger's seat.

Tracy blinked. "What time is it?"

He looked at his watch. "Seven fifteen."

"Sheesh." Tracy checked her center consul for her keys, then the top of the dashboard.

"I like your dress," he said. "Good color."

"It's a skirt," she said. "A dress is if it's all connected. This is a shirt plus a skirt. I sewed the skirt myself." She pointed to them. "Shirt, skirt," she said.

"Shirt, skirt," he said.

He nodded toward the shoe box sitting next to her. "Sorry about your father."

"Thanks," Tracy said. "Here we are," she said. Her keys were underneath the box.

"I love snow," the German said, running his hand along the side-view mirror of her truck so that a small pile gathered at his fingertip.

Tracy gazed out the windshield. She wondered if they were getting snow in Onekama and if the graveyard at St. Mary's on the lake had been shoveled. She pictured her father's headstone not as a stone at all, but as one small, anonymous white mound in a silent and snow-covered cemetery.

Tracy turned the key in the ignition. The heater rattled and whirred and the book on tape started back up.

"Shirt, skirt," the German said, while he eased the door shut beside Tracy. "Shirt, skirt, shirt, skirt."

SOMETHING ELSE

Snowflakes splashed against the windshield of her truck, and Tracy tightened her posture against her seat. She slipped off her work heels at a red light and massaged the arch of her left foot over the brake pedal. Chef had just sent everyone home, announcing that they wouldn't open for dinner service on account of the forecast. Tracy would have preferred to work, even on a slow night; she was hurting for cash after the holidays.

On the other hand, she thought, it might be nice to watch the Bills game at home by herself. Apparently Greenie was now dating one of the Buffalo Jills, and the staff members at the restaurant were all gossipy about that, pointing her out on television every time there was a game, commenting on her figure. Tracy wondered if Greenie considered this girl "marriage material." She hadn't spoken to him since Thanksgiving. She couldn't stomach the thought of him with one of those tiny, bouncing, high-ponytailed girls.

The weather got worse as Tracy continued south, toward home. Traffic slowed to a near standstill. The plows hadn't yet come through. The SUV in front of Tracy put on their hazards and the yellow headlights of oncoming traffic wormed slowly past.

Tracy lost control of her truck when she reached the intersection of Route 5 and Lakeshore. She had overcompensated her acceleration up a small rise and into the shoulder, and here the road veered gently to the left to match the curvature of the lake. As she rounded the turn, Tracy felt her tires lose their grip beneath her. She stomped her brake hard with her heel and the truck shivered with resistance, but couldn't correct itself on the slick road. The back end of her pickup slowly spun out in a wide angle, pulling the entire vehicle off the road so that the rear bumper smacked and groaned against the guardrail, and the back end of the truck lodged deep into the ditch.

It all happened slowly, allowing Tracy to process each jolt and impact as it took place, and she knew instantly when her truck came to rest that there would be no getting it out. The truck was tilted sharply nose up, the back end completely buried and the rear bumper resting heavy on the guardrail. *Dammit*, she breathed as she pulled her key from the ignition. She didn't have her cell phone on her; she'd neglected to charge it before work so hadn't bothered taking it at all. She peered out the windshield. No one had stopped her in passing, and there was no oncoming traffic that she could see.

She peered across the road and in toward the nearest home. The lights were on.

She passed this house on her daily commute. It was the biggest and most impressive in Lakeside Terrace, a grand rolling development, with a view of the lake and a small fishpond out front, a perky little fountain that had probably been winterized and wasn't visible now beneath the snow. The house itself was big and bland and effortful in a new-money, 1990s kind of way. It was both tall and vast, made of sandy-colored brick with small areas of beige siding, the roof varied with dozens of tiers and angles. Three ivory pillars decorated the front porch, and two large lantern-style lights illuminated the double-paned glass doors. Tracy had often admired the place. It was the kind of home that she imagined she would live in if things had worked out with the orthodontist.

Tracy turned off her hazards. She put her shoes back on, pulled the hood of her coat up around her face, and gathered her purse and keys and AAA information from her glove compartment. She got out of the truck and locked it. She struggled up the bank, through a tall drift, and across the road. The snow was so thick that already the tracks from her truck had blown over and nearly disappeared. The wind was razor sharp. Her work heels weren't fit for a hike through this kind of snow and she could feel moisture make its way in to her toes.

On the far side of the road, she lost her footing upon reaching the ditch. She slid on her heels and fell to her bottom, catching herself with the hand that also held her purse. The wet snow immediately penetrated her clothing and she could feel moisture on her ass, the back of her knees, up the sleeves of her winter coat to the bones of her elbows.

She got to her feet and dusted the snow off of her purse. She held it against her chest and proceeded toward the house. Lights were on and a grand tree decorated with red garland and gently twinkling white lights was placed directly in front of the floor-to-ceiling window near the entrance. She reached the front door and rang the bell, a tiny silver electronic thing, and she could hear its melody faintly through the glass door.

The chill quickly spread to her stomach where it felt hard and sad and lonely. She held herself and shivered.

A kid answered the door. He wasn't wearing pants. He had on a white Buffalo Bills T-shirt over light blue boxers, and a pair of men's suede slippers that hung two inches beyond his heel. He was skinny and sandy-haired and pimply. His eyes were small and the whites were cloudy and yellowish but the blue iris was very bright. The warmth of the house met Tracy's face and softened it.

"Hola," Tracy said. She was shivering from her waist and her lips wouldn't meet.

The kid stared at her.

She took her hand from her pocket and jerked her thumb backward over her shoulder in the direction of her truck. "I'm in a ditch," she said.

The kid wasn't tall enough to see over her shoulder, so she stepped to the side so he could gaze out around her.

"I don't have my phone on me," she explained.

The kid looked back at Tracy. A painful-looking pimple rose from the direct center of his chin, like it had been placed there as a challenge. The kid's slim shoulders trembled with cold. She could see his left nipple through his T-shirt. He was holding a tumbler with an inch of caramel-colored liquid in it and several tinkling ice cubes.

"You wanna come in or something?" His voice was lower than she expected—he sounded more man than boy.

Tracy nodded. She followed him into the house and stood on the mauve doormat as the kid reached behind her to pull the door shut.

A grand marble banister bisected the entryway; the stairway was wide and curved to nearly a right angle so that she couldn't see exactly how far up it went and what lay at the top. The handrail was black iron with ornate posts. Fake ivy was spiraled neatly around it the whole way up. A Tiffany chandelier lit the vast chamber. It was silent as a tomb.

It was easily the most impressive house Tracy had ever set foot inside. It looked like the places they featured on those television shows about celebrity homes. She found it hard to believe a place like this could exist a mere three or four miles from her own home.

"Take off your shoes," the kid said.

Tracy was taken aback by his tone, but figured it was a house rule, and she wrestled her heels off with her toes. She placed them neatly at the edge of the rug. Her stockings were soaked. She was still wearing her winter coat, and she pushed the hood back from her face. The fake fur that lined her hood was ratty and smelled like cigarettes and a barn.

"You wanna use my phone?" the kid said. There was no upholstery in the entryway, and his voice reverberated as though they were in an empty chapel.

"I guess," Tracy said. "Your folks around?"

"Nope." The kid stepped behind Tracy to lock the door both at its brass knob, as well as the deadbolt six inches above it. He kicked off his own shoes, then went to the banister where he set the tumbler on the bottom step, then leapt up the stairs in quick rabbit strides, skipping every other one.

Tracy's sleeves were sopping wet from the snow, and clung to her wrists like cold slugs. She pulled the AAA book from her pocket. She flipped through the book to locate the number for weather-related emergencies and stuck her index finger in it to hold the page. Tracy peered at the tumbler on the bottom step, went to it, and leaned her nose in over the glass to investigate. Her face immediately woke to the sting of alcohol at her nostrils.

She blinked and straightened up and walked softly to her right, where the entryway opened to the living room. It was immaculate, with rose-colored carpet, dark cherry furnishings, gauzy curtains. A china cabinet to her left held rows of porcelain and pewter and carnival glass plates, displayed on little wooden stands with legs. Across the room, a painting of a black Labrador with a pheasant in its mouth hung above the piano. Huge framed photographs of kids with serious expressions rested on the fireplace mantel. The fire lapped upward from fake charred logs in even, controlled flames. The couch and loveseat were matching cream-colored leather, and an enormous flat-screen occupied nearly an entire wall. The television was on and an advertisement for a collection of literature on Christian marriage was playing, muted.

Tracy was startled by the sudden clang of a cowbell and quickly turned to her sharp left, where she noticed a six-foot-tall birdcage on the far side of the china cabinet. She took several steps toward the cage. It was made of bamboo, with a domed top and several perches within it. It smelled vaguely of cedar. The cowbell swayed on a thick silver chain. A waist-high tray held both a Tupperware container with some reddish crumbs, and a stuffed yellow mouse with a shredded tail. The bird was perched on the far side of the cage, staring motionless at Tracy and gripping the side of the cage with its talons. It was remarkably big, football-sized, cobalt blue with gold in its beak and circling both eyes.

"It's a hyacinth macaw." The kid was suddenly at Tracy's side and he gazed in at the bird. He said in a rather nasty tone, "Thinks he's such a smarty. His name's Simon. He's my stepdad's."

The bird turned his head to face the kid and blinked once.

"Does he talk?" Tracy asked.

"A little." The kid looked in at the bird. "Do you talk?"

The bird said, "A little," in an unpleasant squawk. He readjusted his talons around his perch and bobbed his head up and down.

"What else do you say?" Tracy asked the bird.

The bird made a high-pitched catcall whistle and exclaimed, "You're something else!"

Tracy laughed.

The kid said, "He says that to everyone."

The kid offered his cell phone to Tracy. He had remarkable fingernails for a kid, she thought; perfectly clean, evenly cut, and with smooth edges as though they'd been filed. Tracy took the phone and stared at it in her hand for a moment, thumbing the smooth, even plane of a screen with no keyboard.

"One of them iPhones?" she said. Most of the young staff members at the restaurant used these, but she'd never even laid a hand on one.

The kid snatched it back from her and quickly pulled up a dial pad.

Tracy entered the AAA number and was put on hold. She watched the bird clean himself beneath its wings, snapping at his feathers with his beak and waggling his head back and forth. The dispatcher who finally answered her call said it might be up to two or three hours until they'd get someone out there. Roads were bad all over the county and they had a long lineup of folks in need of help.

Tracy hung up and reported this to the kid, then she tapped the corner of the phone against her chin. "Well, now I can't think who else to call," she said.

"Aren't you married?" the kid said.

"No."

"Why not?"

"Geez oh Pete," Tracy said.

"No friends?" The kid didn't seem suspicious nor particularly concerned, just casually intrigued by this idea.

"Yeah, I've got friends," Tracy said. "I don't keep their numbers memorized. Do you have a phone book or something?"

The kid laughed. "A *phone book*?" He took his phone back from her.

He used the bottom inch of his T-shirt to wipe the screen of his phone. "I don't care if you hang out here," he said. "My stepdad Kevin, he's a real prick, but he can probably help you with your truck, him and my mom will be home in an hour or two."

Tracy considered this. "That's a little weird, don't you think?"

The kid shrugged. "No," he said. "I don't think it's that weird. I don't think it's weird at all." He nodded into the living room. "I'm just watching TV."

"I'm Tracy, by the way," she said.

"Charlie."

Tracy shivered from the base of her spine. Her hands were still waxy pink and puffy from the cold.

Charlie said, "Do you want to borrow something of my mom's so you can warm up? She wouldn't care." He stared at Tracy's body for a moment and said, "I think you're about the same size."

Tracy weighed the offer and tried to place herself in Charlie's mother's shoes. She wasn't sure if she'd want just any old stranger off the street wearing one of her outfits. On the other hand, she was sure to get sick if she didn't dry off and warm up. She'd want to be hospitable to someone in her position.

"My mom's really nice," Charlie insisted. "I'm sure she wouldn't care."

Tracy pointed toward the tumbler, still resting on the bottom step of the staircase. "Would your stepdad care that you're drinking his whiskey?"

Charlie jerked his head around and scowled at her. "It's bourbon. And I'd say that's none of your business. Especially after I let you in my house and all." His adolescent voice honked like a clarinet.

Tracy made a little noise with her tongue on the roof of her mouth. "I just don't wanna be part of any bad scene or anything."

• • •

Charlie returned with a pair of fleecy pajama pants, a pale yellow T-shirt, and wool socks in a neat pile. He showed Tracy to the downstairs bathroom. It was spotless with a classic beachy theme; a conch shell for a soap dish, coconut hand soap, the bathmat sky blue. Tracy took off her own clothing and spread it over the shower rod. She dried herself completely with a plushy hand towel, until all her goose bumps had retreated, before dressing herself in Charlie's mother's clothing.

She was tying the ribbon belt of the pajama pants at her waist when she thought she saw a shadow pass directly beneath the bathroom door. Her breath snagged suddenly against the back of her throat like she'd swallowed a hair. She glanced at the handle to make sure she had locked the door, then pressed her ear to it. The only sound she could hear was the faraway prattling of the television in the other room. The shadow was nothing; she'd only spooked herself.

The yellow shirt was thinner than she'd have liked, and both garments fit too tightly. She grasped the shirt in her fists and pulled it out from her body in handfuls to stretch the thing out. She wished she was wearing a white bra rather than her cheapo one with the red plaid pattern, which showed clearly through the shirt. She did lunges in the pants so that they would accommodate her ass. She had a great body for her age, men in bars said so all the time, but she reckoned she was a good two or three sizes larger than Charlie's mom. She imagined that Charlie's mom, living in a house like this and all, probably did a lot of yoga and drank a lot of green juice.

• • •

Charlie had poured Tracy both a glass of water and a glass of bourbon when she returned to the living room. She took a seat at the far end of the leather couch, which sank generously beneath her as though it had been holding its breath in anticipation of her. Charlie was watching the television intently. A televangelist stood at center stage, and the rumbling of an audience bellowed from surround sound. The screen was so large the man was eight feet tall. A line of audience members gathered in front of the preacher, who held a woman's face in his hands.

Tracy had only ever passed this channel en route to other shows; she'd never watched more than ten seconds of a program like this. She thought it was horseshit. She took a seat next to Charlie. His fists were clenched like he was watching a sporting event.

The camera panned in on the preacher. He wore a gray pin-stripe suit and gold tie. His face was frighteningly large and detailed on the high-definition screen; cheeks flaming with rosacea and a very intense expression. He clutched a woman at the sides of her face, and murmured. Her long blond braid swung free and low behind her.

"Here she goes," Charlie whispered. Tracy glanced sideways at him. His whole body was tense like he was about to jump out of his seat.

"Here she goes," he said again. "Watch this."

The woman on the television convulsed and then wilted into the arms of two broad and muscular men behind her, her braid dropping so low it grazed the ground. The preacher gyrated briefly, and gestured for the next person to come forward as the woman was carried away.

"I LOVE this guy!" Charlie said. "Don't you *love* this guy?"

Tracy stared at him.

"He's the best in the business," Charlie offered. "The business of hypnosis, I mean."

"How do you mean?"

"I've read all about it. These guys are all trained hypnotists. You can talk people into anything when they're under a spell."

Tracy said, "I've seen that movie about the hypnotist. The one from the nineties. You seen that? Pretty scary stuff."

"Wanna see something? Follow me." Charlie walked her over to Simon's cage.

He stood in front of the cage and whistled at the bird. Simon snapped his head to the side and tittered beneath one of his wings. He puffed his chest out. He looked directly at Tracy for a moment and shrieked, "You're something else!"

Charlie said, "Can you move out of his line of sight?"

Tracy stepped to her left.

Charlie became very still and caught the bird's gaze. He shushed the bird. Simon hopped over to the edge of the cage on his perch. Dust swirled around a single exposed lightbulb at the top of his cage and in this spotlight, he was electric blue. Charlie murmured, "Sleepy, sleepy," to the bird.

Simon said, "Sleepy, sleepy," back to Charlie, and snapped his beak a little bit.

Charlie said, "Sleepy, sleepy," again, in a very low and calm whisper. He raised his hand to wave very slowly, extending his fingers one at a time in a relaxed and mesmerizing pattern. Simon followed the hand with his eyes. He blinked once and cocked his head, then blinked again, very slowly. "Sleepy, sleepy," Charlie said. Simon's body teetered and swayed to the left.

"Sleepy," said Charlie again. "Shhhh."

Tracy watched in amazement as the bird toppled left off his perch, like dead weight, his body stiff. Simon wakened when he thunked to the floor of the cage. He quickly stood and ruffled his wings and opened his beak in what looked like a yawn.

"That was incredible," Tracy said. She couldn't take her eyes off the bird.

"Not bad, eh?" Charlie looked very pleased.

They returned to the television, where the healing segment had ended and it now showed a woman reading scripture and talking directly to the camera, a hotline number sweeping across the bottom of the screen. Charlie picked up the remote and changed the channel to ESPN.

Tracy nodded down toward the stack of cork Buffalo Bills coasters. "You like the Bills?"

"Yeah," said Charlie. "You?"

Tracy nodded. "Lived here all my life. My granddad played for them until he injured his knee."

"Cool," said Charlie. "You get to lots of games?"

"Nah," Tracy said, "I've actually never been. But I'm saving up to go this fall. The Bills-Patriots game. I'm saving up for a really good seat, gonna sit sideline."

She and Greenie had often talked about going to a game together but it had never worked out—he always complained about the price or had a scheduling conflict. She wondered now if the Buffalo Jill would be able to get him free tickets.

Charlie made an indifferent little frown. "It's not that cool," he said. "I've sat in the lower-level seats a couple times with Kevin. It's hard to follow what's going on. I'd rather just watch on TV." He picked at a thread in the bottom seam of his T-shirt. "So where do you live?" he asked.

"Southtowns. It's the pits compared to here."

"I know the Southtowns," Charlie said. "It's where we lived til my dad and mom split up. Our old house is right next to that boarded-up Blockbuster on Eleven."

"Sure," said Tracy. "I know right where that is."

Charlie made an ugly face. "You live close to there?"

"Not too far," Tracy said. "I'm on the lake side."

Charlie polished off the rest of his drink, and stood. "You want some food?"

"Sure," said Tracy.

Charlie returned a moment later with a bag of chips and two milkshakes.

The bird whistled at Charlie when he passed the cage.

Charlie said, "Shut up, Simon."

Tracy drank her milkshake. The pregame show broke for commercials and Tracy rose to clean their glasses. Charlie followed her into the kitchen and gazed out the kitchen window before them while Tracy started to rinse the glasses.

"What position did your granddad play?" he said.

"Running back," Tracy said. "Banged up his knee real bad in his first season though. Never played again."

Their sink had one of those fancy mobile faucet heads, and

Tracy grasped and drew it back from the sink on its metallic cord, which flexed generously. She turned on the water, and it shot out in a violent stream, hitting the base of the sink with such surprising force that it flew from her hand. It wiggled for a second in the base of the sink, righting itself into its back so the water sprayed out straight and true, into the air, onto her, onto Charlie, before she could reach the handle to turn it off. She wiped her face with her forearm.

Charlie was scowling. His bangs were wet and shaped differently. He looked younger.

"I'm sorry," she said. "I never use this kind of faucet. I'm sorry."

Charlie stuck an index finger directly into his right eyeball.

"Are you OK?" she said.

"My contact came out."

"Really?"

"*Ow*." He rubbed at his face.

"Here, let's take a look around you," Tracy said, crouching to the ground without repositioning her feet, so as not to step on the thing.

"How do you think I'm gonna look for it?" Charlie snapped.

"Here, if we just get down close to the ground like this maybe the light will catch it. I'll look around my feet all the way to the baseboard, you look around yours."

"No, I mean how do you think I'm gonna *look*," he said. "It's my freakin' contact. I'm totally blind without it. Practically legally blind."

Tracy knelt to her hands and knees now, her kneecaps grinding painfully into the hardwood floors. She scoured the floor with her eyes, moving them back and forth across the floor in broad, efficient patterns. She grazed the surface of the floor with her fingers.

"I don't see a thing," Tracy said.

"Maybe you need better light." Charlie directed her toward a drawer where she retrieved a flashlight and used it to scan beneath the lip of the cabinets near them, then once again across the floorboards.

"You're sure it didn't float up higher on your eyeball?" she said. "I don't see it anywhere."

"Yeah, I'm sure it's not in there. I'd feel it."

Back and forth Tracy went with the sweeping beam of the flashlight, then again without it. She shuffled slowly from one end of the kitchen to the other. She examined the counter and the front edge of the cabinets. She placed her cheek on the ground to examine the floor at surface level.

Charlie said, "What are you doing?"

"Trying to get the best angle to look," Tracy said.

"Oh, OK," Charlie said. "I thought you were resting. I don't want you to stop until you find it." Charlie was swaying mildly back and forth. She wondered if he was drunk.

Tracy knelt back down and continued to scan the ground.

After a minute or two she said, "Look, Charlie, I'm sorry. I don't think I'm gonna find it. I'm sorry. Don't you have glasses or something you can wear?"

"No," he said. "Keep looking."

Once again, Tracy swept gently across the slick hardwood, running her fingers along the grain and then against it. She examined Charlie's shoes.

"Is it one of the soft kind?" she said. "Big and cupped?"

Charlie nodded.

"Well, where on earth . . ." Tracy returned to her hands and knees.

When the sound of Simon's shrill catcall whistle from the other room broke a chilly silence, Tracy suddenly realized she had completely lost track of the time she had been on the ground. She had no clue if she'd been looking for that contact for five minutes or three hours. Her lower back was screaming, as though she'd been in that position for days. She leaned back so her butt could rest on her heels for a moment.

She looked up at Charlie. He was staring intensely at her.

"My back's killing me," she said.

Charlie's posture softened and he blinked. He stepped back toward the sink, poured himself a glass of water, and took a sip from it. "It's no big deal," he said.

Tracy sat uncomfortably in the loveseat and massaged her knees while Charlie arranged a throw blanket around his legs and hummed something cheerful. Simon was shuffling around in his cage. Tracy slid an Eddie Bauer catalogue out from the small wooden rack at her side and gazed for several minutes at pictures of smiling people in turtlenecks and shearling boots.

A commercial for Ford Explorers played quietly on the television. It showed an SUV charging up a steep and snowy pass. Tracy thought of her truck and hoped it wouldn't need any repairs once it had been dug out of the ditch. Charlie gazed at the digital clock on the cable box and said, "It's a quarter to seven. The Bills game should start soon, right?"

Tracy glanced over toward the cable box as well. She couldn't quite make out the numbers on the clock to confirm the time—they were a blurred little streak of yellowy green.

She tried to look back at the television nonchalantly, but couldn't avoid Charlie's gaze, which was now on her. His eyes glittered like clarified jewels and she understood now that he was seeing her perfectly, that his vision was fine, that he couldn't possibly be "nearly blind," as he'd said, without contacts. If he could read the time on that clock, he probably didn't even wear contacts at all. There was an ominous feeling cradled in her stomach. Why had he tricked her?

Charlie turned back toward the TV and said nonchalantly, "I'm gonna make another drink before the game starts. Do you want one?"

Tracy nodded quickly and tried to maintain a relaxed posture as he left the room. She absently leaned forward, this time reaching for the sketchpad that sat on the lower level of the coffee table in front of her.

The sketchpad fell open before her, and now she felt something like a cold blast whoosh through her. She was overcome by the sudden and unshakable knowledge that something very bad was at work.

She stared down at a detailed drawing of her own face, and her mind flew, processing information in harsh and senseless thunderclaps. The drawing was chillingly, remarkably accurate. Eraser marks indicated edits, a long time spent on the piece to perfect it. The shading was just right. Her hair messy and large, as it was now. How had he done this without her noticing? She considered that strange, gray period of time that had elapsed as she knelt helplessly on the kitchen floor, taking orders from him. That black hole of time wherein she simply could not recall what had passed, though she'd had the distinct impression that many minutes had been lost. In the picture, her eyes stared directly into the eyes of the artist. The expression on her face in the drawing was empty, trusting, and vaguely childlike; an expression she'd never before seen upon her own face, and this made her tremble as though she'd been horribly violated. She realized that she had absolutely no idea what this boy was capable of.

Tracy leapt up from the couch, the sketchpad falling to her feet. Her heart was slamming in her ears. She crept soundlessly to the front door, her legs too small and weak to support the rest of her. She couldn't tell if the cold wet on her face was from tears or perspiration. She grabbed her winter coat and stuffed her arms through the damp sleeves. She was reaching for her shoes when Simon's shrill whistle cut through the room. "You're something else!" the bird called.

"*Shit*, Simon!" Tracy hissed, bolting back to the living room and to the birdcage, where she unlatched the door with trembling fingers and pulled it open. She stuck her hand inside.

"Come on," she whispered to the bird, and she realized now that these were hot tears pulsing on her face. She held out an index finger, which trembled violently at the bird's feet. She patted her forearm. "Come *on*, Simon," she whispered again to the bird. He blinked and cocked his head for a second before reluctantly stepping onto her arm one foot at a time. His talons were cold and sharp on her skin. He nipped at her wrist a little bit.

She couldn't hear anything over the blood in her head. She secured him to her chest, inside her winter coat, with her left hand, and raced back toward the front door. The bird struggled against her chest and Tracy felt his talons ripping at her shirt. She wanted to scream but it was like she had swallowed a perfectly sized stopper.

Tracy didn't worry about the noise she made as she unlocked the deadbolt—she was too close to waste time being quiet now. Her heart was beating painfully. She didn't bother with her heels either—she knew she would get farther faster without them. The deadbolt unlatched internally with a heavy clunk, and below it, the lock on the knob itself disengaged and opened smoothly.

She flung the door open and was met by a mighty rush of delicious cold oxygen, which surged into her lungs and tickled them. She ran through snow, not taking any care to stay on the walkway, just running wildly in the wool socks, which quickly soaked through, leaving her toes numb and hard. Simon was tucked close to her chest inside her winter coat, only his little blue head exposed. He picked at her collar with his beak. She thought she heard him whistle at her. It occurred to her that Simon might freeze to death before they reached the next house, and that she might too for that matter, yet still this seemed somehow better than what might eventually happen to them at Charlie's. Were his parents coming home tonight? Did he even have parents?

She stumbled over a bank of snow and righted herself just as she could make out a soft yellowy smudge in dark horizon, which she knew to be the street light at the corner Shell station. She wondered who she might find there. She wondered if Simon would still be alive. She wondered what Charlie would do with his drawing of her, what else was in that sketchbook, and what

Charlie's mother would make of the clothing that was hung neatly over the shower curtain in her downstairs restroom: a collared shirt from Target with fake pearl buttons, a pair of black stockings with a dime-sized hole in the toe, and a handmade black chiffon skirt with vertical citrine stripes.

THE SNOWY TREE CRICKET

Jim had just finished a twelve-hour shift, starting at 6:00 a.m. The sky was charcoal to the east and magenta to the west. Jim had grown fonder of Butte over time, and now he admired the mountains of the Anaconda-Pintler range, still snow-covered, that rose far beyond the city, and out in the other direction, the ninety-foot-tall statue of the Virgin Mary, which sat atop the Continental Divide. Our Lady of the Rockies, they called her, and she was illuminated so that she could be seen from any point in Butte at any time of day or night. Jim had hiked out to her lonely perch to see her up close once, and was most impressed with the indifference of her. From the city, her arms were warmly outstretched and inviting, all of her angles gentle and motherly, but up close, she was as cool and expressionless as any old chunk of concrete.

Jim had decided to forego an invitation to an orientation dinner tonight, for some of the new hires. He was usually up for a free meal, but tonight he was beat. He thought back to his own orientation dinner, when he had met another transplant from the Buffalo area. The guy was very tall, strong-shouldered and soft-spoken. "Small world," Jim remarked to the guy upon finding out where he was from, and the guy agreed. The guy's last job, before working for the food plant, had been in construction, on the expansion of the Seneca Casino. "*No kidding*," Jim said. "I was there the night they reopened the casino. You probably were too, huh? We coulda sat at the same table and everything. You a blackjack guy?"

The guy introduced himself as Cole, but Jim noticed, a moment later when he retrieved a single from his wallet to tip the bar, that his driver's license said something different. The guy had ordered an O'Doul's, and Jim commented that he ought to do the same, if he knew what was good for himself. They talked Buffalo for a minute, then Butte. The guy was living outside of town, in a duplex that overlooked the massive Berkley pit. The pit hadn't been mined since the eighties, but it was a real sight, with its variegated stone walls and blue-gold water. Jim said, "Creepy-lookin' water, if you ask me. I reckon if there's any such thing as the Loch Ness, it's livin' in a place like that."

Later that night, they sat next to one another at the High Horse.

Jim drank too much, and couldn't remember a word of their conversation, but he woke the next morning feeling very strange. Different. He desperately tried to assemble a memory of the evening. What had been said? He could not recall. He clapped his hands over the pockets of his khakis, which he'd neglected to change out of. His pockets were empty—no clues.

He didn't cross paths with Cole once at the plant that week, and wondered if perhaps Cole worked the night shift. Jim tried to look him up in the company directory, but there was no one listed by that name. He asked the bartender at the High Horse if Cole had been back since that night, and the bartender thought not.

The following week, Jim attended his first-ever AA meeting, hoping to find Cole there.

Cole was not at the meeting, but Jim liked the other guys who were. Good guys, plainspoken, and Jim started to attend meetings regularly. He also started to cook for himself so that he could avoid the temptation of a whiskey with dinner at the High Horse. He became quite good at cooking. He started to sleep better too. The physical demands of the job were such that by the end of the day, Jim was satisfied by an hour of television, a good meal, and an early bedtime.

Although he initially didn't care much for Butte, over time Jim came to like the town a lot. Downtown was hilly and historic with beautiful three-story, falling-apart homes and cracked sidewalks. The faraway mountains were unlike any he'd seen in the east. One night, he bypassed a barbed-wire fence and numerous "No Trespassing" signs to access one of the nearby head frames above an old mine shaft. He climbed the head frame, and the shabby little steps groaned and threatened to crumble beneath him. His heart raced. Ten stories up he climbed, to reach the platform at the top. From here, he admired the lights of Butte while sucking in cold altitude and adrenaline.

This place was not so bad, Jim thought. Not so bad at all. Folks here were friendly. Diner coffee was served in plain white Styrofoam cups. Outside the city of Butte were massive ranch properties with red horses and longhorn cattle. It felt to Jim very much like he was living in the Wild West. He mentioned this in an email to Charlie, and offered to pay for Charlie to make a trip out. Money wasn't an issue, Charlie had said, but he never got back with any dates.

After six months in Butte, Jim had some trouble with his shoulder and needed surgery. He'd no longer be able to do the loading and heavy lifting required by his current position. So, the company offered him a job driving trucks and paid for his CDL training and certification. The money was better, and Jim got sent all up and down the West Coast and into the Rockies.

Jim was doing well. He was saving money, seeing the world. He had lost a little weight. He remembered Charlie's birthday and sent a card *on time* as well as calling on the day. He created an online dating profile and went on a few dates. They weren't spectacular or anything, but he didn't make a fool of himself either. He hadn't made a drunken phone call to Laura in ages. Jim felt A-OK about life. He could hardly believe it. It felt as though he was trying on happiness like it was a garment; to see if it fit, to see if it was worth holding on to.

As Jim paused to scan the stack of the day's mail, his eyes fell upon handwriting that he recognized before he'd even glanced at the return address. Laura wrote with a tight, backward-sloped cursive and grandiose capital letters at the beginning of each line.

The envelope was a padded eight-by-twelve bubble mailer with a cluster of American flag stamps in the corner. Jim examined the front and back of this envelope. There was a scribbly little circle of pen on the backside, where Laura had likely tested it out to make sure it would write on this surface. The corners were soft, as though it had not been handled carefully. Jim set it on top of the rest of his mail, which contained a utilities bill and a passel of coupons for the Eagle supermarket.

Jim parked his car in the spot directly out front of his home and carried the mail and his empty Nalgene bottle inside to his kitchen table. He was exhausted from the long workday, but this letter from Laura had his heart leaping. When she sent legal documents, it was always either via email, or through her lawyer and directly from that office. He could not think of a time in the last eight years that he'd received personal mail from her. He tossed the rest of the mail aside, and used a butter knife to slip open the envelope from Laura, adrenaline sailing off the top of his head. He tried to prepare himself for both the best and the worst. He could not imagine what either one would entail.

Jim eagerly drew out the contents of the envelope and stared down at what was not a letter, but a drawing.

He fought an immediate hot swell of bile.

He hadn't seen the other woman in over a decade, not once since Laura had found out about their relationship, but the face was instantly recognizable. The drawing was crude and hurried in places, but very skilled overall; the important details and angles of her face rendered perfectly, the left eyebrow arched higher than the right, deep, dark eyes, full lips, hard jawbone. The resemblance to its subject was as clear and obvious as if it had been a photograph. In the lower right corner of the drawing was the scribbled signature of the artist: C. A. McNamara.

A deep and punishing blush quickly warmed Jim's whole head. Charlie Andrew, his son.

Was this a joke? *Ten years* since Jim had last seen this woman's face. Never once in these ten years had he expected that he'd ever see it again. Jim thoughtlessly wound up and swatted the Nalgene bottle squarely from the table so that it flew into the cabinets across the room. It bounced to the floor then rolled very slowly toward the dishwasher, the sound of the bottle against the floor as loud as a train in Jim's ears. The heat on Jim's face traveled downward, settling in his chest, where it thumped with fresh humiliation.

This shame was momentarily interrupted by legitimate confusion. Laura had never seen this other woman's face, had never even known her full name. She had put the pieces together in other ways; catching Jim in lies regarding his whereabouts, bar tabs, unfamiliar smells on him. When she confronted Jim, he told her, truthfully, that he didn't even know the other woman's last name. Laura had insisted several times that Jim must deliver her to the other woman's house so that they could have it out there, all three of them at once, but she seemed to lose interest in this confrontation after a short while, and never followed through on these threats. In fact, it had occurred to Jim at the time, Laura was so quick to end the marriage that Jim honestly thought not only had she stopped caring who the other woman was, but was perhaps even *grateful* to the other woman for providing an excuse to end the marriage.

And, Jim reasoned now, if Laura didn't know who the other woman was, there was *no way* Charlie could have somehow identified her, figured it out on his own, all these years later. No way. And yet, here was her face, this other woman, drawn in his son's own hand.

This was an impossibly cruel scenario, and as Jim stared at the picture now, stupefied, he was further distressed to realize that didn't even know who to blame. Had Laura decided to punish him further, to taunt him? But *why*, after all these years? And . . . *how*? How had Laura found this woman, and why had she involved Charlie? Why had Charlie been forced to stare at this face, to reproduce it with his own hand?

A knock at Jim's door startled him.

Jesus Christ. He was shaking. He pounded the underside of both fists into the table and it vibrated hard beneath him. He felt the vibration in his toes. He wiped his forehead into the crease of his elbow.

The knock came again. And he could've easily ignored it, had it not come from the side door, which entered to the kitchen. Someone who knew him, knew where to enter, could see the light on inside, could probably even see his silhouette. *Jesus Christ*. Jim turned the picture facedown on his kitchen table and went to the door.

Carly, the kid from the next house over, and her little brother, the toddler whose name Jim could never remember, were at the door. Carly balanced her brother on her tiny hip. Both of them were golden-haired and gray-eyed. Carly was a nice kid. Her mother was nice too, but a discouraging sort; ill-fitting workout clothes, noisy fights on the phone with collections agencies. Their house always smelled vaguely sulfuric. Carly was wearing overalls now, and a purple turtleneck. The toddler was chewing on a pacifier but looking otherwise quite serious and grown-up.

"Hi, Mr. McNamara," Carly said.

"What's up?" Jim said irritably. Ordinarily he would have invited them in for lemonade or a snack, but the picture there on his table had him jumping out of his skin, and he didn't want anyone in his house right now. He was afraid of what he was feeling, what he might say.

Carly set her brother down, placing him carefully on his little orange-socked feet, but he quickly bounced down to his bottom and took a seat, slapping his hands on Jim's linoleum floor. Carly pulled a SpongeBob backpack from around her back to her front, and walked it in to Jim's kitchen table to unzip it. She withdrew a Ziploc baggie that held something large, and she thumped it heavily onto his table.

"Banana bread," she said.

The inside of the bag was sweating. The bread was still warm.

"Thanks," Jim said. He felt like crying.

"Hey, you've got a cricket," Carly said.

"What?"

"Didn't you hear it, just there? A cricket this time of year . . . it must've lived in your house all winter long," she said, curiously. "Usually they hibernate til May or June, but he must've stayed with you all winter, to be up and chirping like that. You haven't heard him before?"

Jim considered this for a moment. "I don't believe so."

"Wait for it . . ." Carly said, putting her finger to her lips.

They were silent for a few seconds, and the chirp returned. It sounded like the thing was in the cupboard beneath his sink. Jim couldn't believe he hadn't noticed it before, if in fact it had spent the whole winter there, as Carly suggested.

"I think it's a snowy tree cricket," she said. "These things can tell you the temperature, ya know."

"How's that?" Jim said.

"If you count the number of chirps in fourteen seconds," Carly explained, "And add forty, you've got the number of degrees Fahrenheit. We learned that one in science."

"Is that right?"

"See for yourself," she said.

Jim looked down at his digital watch, and changed the mode to a stopwatch setting. "I'll time it," he said to Carly. "You count."

They stood quietly, listening for the chirp of the snowy tree cricket, and when it returned, Jim started the watch. He waited fourteen seconds, then signaled Carly to stop counting.

"Twenty-eight," she said.

Jim pointed toward his digital thermostat on the wall, and Carly bounded over to check out the temperature on the little display panel. "Sixty-eight degrees," she read out loud.

Jim felt utterly, uncommonly relieved by this—relieved to learn that the snowy tree cricket could be trusted.

He thanked Carly, and told her to thank her mother for the banana bread too. She lugged her brother back up onto her hip, and they left.

Jim sat back down at the kitchen table. He rested both palms on top of the warm loaf firmly, as though feeling for a pulse, preparing to perform CPR on the thing.

He'd call one of them right now, he decided, either Laura or Charlie, get to the bottom of this picture business, hash it out. There was no use putting it off. He briefly weighed the pros and cons of both, and decided to try Charlie first. Before reaching for his phone, Jim listened once again for the snowy tree cricket, and he was so relieved, so appreciative, when the chirp finally returned after what felt like a very long silence.

Jim took a seat at his kitchen table and dialed Charlie's cell phone. While the phone rang, he turned the picture over before him so that the empty backside faced upward. He coughed into his fist and his throat felt as though it had shrunk to half of its normal size.

The phone rang several times, then there was a click, and Laura's voice at the other end. "Hello?"

"Laura?"

"Charlie's in his room," she explained. "He left his phone charging here in the kitchen. Normally I wouldn't touch the thing, but I heard it ring, then saw that it was you . . ."

Jim was analyzing her voice for the anger that he expected, but it sounded soft and eager, perhaps a bit uncertain of itself. Perhaps, if he didn't know better, it almost sounded as though she was pleased to hear from him.

"Laura," he said. "That picture you sent me."

Laura didn't respond.

Jim rested his forehead in his open palm. "How did . . ." he started in. "Why did you . . . Why did Charlie . . ." he grappled for the best entry point.

Laura said, "It's a nice picture, isn't it?"

Nice? Was there sarcasm here? If so, where was the victory in her voice? "*Nice*?" Jim said.

"Yeah, *nice*," she repeated. "I knew he'd never send you any of his work on his own. He's so stubborn about sharing his stuff. I thought you'd be impressed."

Jim was speechless.

"Didn't I tell you this in the letter?" Laura continued. "I thought I told you. He was in such a mood last week, saying he was going to burn all his sketchbooks, that it was all garbage, it's always something with him . . . Anyway, I begged him not to trash all of that work. Begged him to let me keep those sketchbooks. He didn't care one way or the other, and handed them over to me. I paged through them and was so im*pressed*, you know? He really doesn't know how good he is. *I* didn't know how good he is. This particular drawing stuck out to me, I don't know, I just like it. I wanted you to see it." She paused. "Didn't I tell you all this in the letter?"

"What letter?"

"The one I sent with the picture, Jim, obviously."

"There was no letter."

"Oh . . ." Laura said, wearily. "Did I forget to put the letter in? I swear . . . Did I forget to send the letter? Here . . . hang on . . . let me see something . . ."

Jim listened to her soft panting as she went up a flight of stairs, then the shuffling of papers.

"Oh, for heaven's sake," Laura said. "Here it is. It was meant to go in with the picture, but I must've absent-mindedly shoved it back into my desk rather than the envelope. I don't know where my head's at, Jim. Really, I don't."

"Wait . . ." Jim said, still reeling, battling disbelief. "Wait . . . Laura, do you know the woman in the picture?"

"What? No," she said, sounding a bit surprised by the question, indifferent to it. "I asked Charlie the same thing, and he said she was just a stranger. He's got lots of pictures of people, you know, strangers. I just happened to like this one in particular, this face. It's a good face."

"I see," said Jim, his brain flooding with both a cool wash of relief, and wonder at the possibility that this picture had come about purely by happenstance. He turned the picture back over in front of him and stared at the face again. Ran his finger over his son's signature in the lower right-hand corner.

"But don't you want to know what's in it?" Laura said.

"What's in what?"

"*The letter*," Laura said, "that I meant to send you. I have it here in front of me now, you want me to read it to you?"

Laura's letter opened with an apology for the time that had elapsed since her last call. She said that she was terribly lonely and worried about Charlie, whose behavior grew more cryptic and dark and unpredictable every day. She knew that she hadn't done much to earn Jim's sympathy, but she didn't know were else to turn, who else might share her concern for Charlie. She said that she missed Jim. Her voice wavered here as she read these words. Jim hiccupped in a half sob, covering his mouth so that she wouldn't know. He longed for her.

Laura started into the next sentence, but then she stopped abruptly.

"Laura?" Jim pressed his ear to the speaker. "Are you there?" he said. "Laura?"

Now Jim could hear a man's voice in the background, and Laura hung up Charlie's phone without saying good-bye.

Jim stared at his phone in his palm as the "Call Ended" screen flashed, then it went blank.

"*Come back*," he whispered.

Jim waited a few minutes, then tried to call Laura, this time on her cell phone, not Charlie's. It went straight to voicemail, as though it had been turned off. He waited a few more minutes, then called again, and this time he left a voicemail. He said he wanted to help. He offered to fly from Butte to Buffalo the very next day. He said that he'd like to hear the rest of the letter. He paused and said that he sure did miss her too.

He sat at the table and tried to replay their entire conversation in his head. He wished he had it recorded. He wanted to know every single word, relive those seconds, her voice. Did she want him in her life again? He didn't dare get his hopes up. Her missing him didn't mean anything more than that. You could miss someone and no longer want them. You could miss them even if the love was gone. *What was in that letter?*

Jim tried to distract himself while he waited to hear back from Laura. He did a load of laundry. He poached a chicken and ate it over spinach. He cut off a slice of the banana bread the neighbor girl had brought over, and ate it with margarine. He checked his phone, email, phone, email, nearly lost his mind when the phone rang and it was not Laura but the guy down the street who had borrowed his power hacksaw.

"Sorry," he said to the guy after answering the phone testily.

"I'm waitin' on a call. You can just drop it by whenever—I'll be up until nine or ten."

Half an hour later, Jim received an email from Laura: *Sorry Jim—it was a mistake to drag you into this. Kevin prefers that we don't speak anymore unless it involves Charlie and is absolutely necessary. Take care.*

Jim read this email, then read it six more times, and once more, aloud, shouting every word.

He desperately wanted a whiskey. This craving was worse than any he'd had in years, and he felt it from his hair to his toenails. He wanted his hand around the neck of a full bottle, wanted to pour it down his throat until he was blind.

He closed his laptop, trembling with the effort of doing so gently. He went to his living room and opened a newspaper. He couldn't focus on a single word. He shredded the newspaper into strips and threw these pieces to the ground. He stuffed a crumpled ball of it into his mouth then spat it out. He hollered into his hands. He got up and punched his fireplace, which left his knuckles raw.

Then, almost instantaneously, he felt much better.

He calmly picked up the pieces of newspaper and put them in his trash can. He ate another slice of banana bread. The guy from down the street returned with his hacksaw and apologized profusely for a small chip in the blade that he believed he'd caused. Jim said he was pretty sure it had been like that before.

At the end of Jim's contract in Butte, in June, it was announced that the plant was only doing so-so, and reductions would be made. So, Jim got sent back to New York, for a need-based job driving trucks out of the Dunkirk plant. He contacted Laura to notify her of his return, and received a very curt response, wishing him well with the move.

Jim rented out a place in the Southtowns and waited for assignments. He was seldom without work for more than a week or two at a time, and during these weeks, he kept himself occupied with online courses in management, and new recipes. He offered to take Charlie out to lunch when Charlie returned his calls, which was not often. When they did spend time together, Charlie kept his head buried in his phone, offering nothing. Jim always hoped to overlap with Laura during the pickup, or drop-off, but this did not occur.

He went to AA meetings whenever he was able. He wondered if Cole had returned to the Buffalo area, if they might cross paths at one of these meetings. With these years of hindsight, it had become clear to Jim that the night he'd met Cole was the night when some inexplicable shift had occurred in his life. Jim still often thought about that night, wishing to understand what had transpired, what had been said in those lost moments. Jim wondered how he'd changed from a man who couldn't hold a five-minute conversation without three drinks in his system, a man who hated himself so much that he sabotaged his own marriage, to a man who could acknowledge all of the things he'd lost, face them head on, a man who could spend Christmas alone and stone-cold sober. How he'd managed to become a man who finally deserved the things he once had.

THE USS CROAKER

Tracy ran her fingernail in small circles over the waxy tablecloth. She looked out the window of the restaurant to a shabby little beach that was empty except for some charred Budweiser cans and a flip-flop stuck upright in the sand. The lake was army green and the water seemed thin and volatile in this heat, like it might take the form of powder if you lifted a handful of it. A motorboat with a faded Buffalo Bills insignia painted on the side bobbed in water that seemed too shallow, and its driver was drinking straight from a two-liter bottle.

"Do you know what you want?" Greenie said.

Tracy ordered water and a six-dollar fish sandwich.

If she had been paying for lunch, she'd have gotten a lemonade too, and the sandwich platter, which included fries and a tiny cup of coleslaw. But since Greenie had already offered to pay, Tracy was determined to order as little as possible. It was their last meal together, and she didn't want him to leave with the impression that he'd been generous with her.

"That was nice of Chef to give you the day off," Greenie said.

Tracy nodded. She raked her fork across her paper napkin. "You all packed up?"

"Yeah," Greenie said.

"Did you have any trouble fitting it all in your car?"

"Nah," he said. "I'm leaving some stuff behind with my folks for now. My TV, and some of my kitchen stuff, which they'll probably destroy. Oh well." Greenie's eyes were pale in the sunshine and his hair was the color of ink.

"What do you mean?"

"My Teflon pans," Greenie said. His mouth was full and he spoke out of one corner of it. "You can't use a metal utensil on a Teflon pan. It scratches it. Ruins the surface. I've explained it to 'em a million times, but they still do it. I'm like, 'Well, I'm pretty sure *I* didn't put those new scratches on my Teflon pan.'"

Tracy had spent the night at Greenie's place once, long ago, when his parents were out of town, and she tried to remember now if she had used a metal fork while preparing eggs in Greenie's Teflon pan.

Greenie was leaving that afternoon for New Jersey, where he would work as the manager at his cousin's new restaurant. He hadn't suggested that Tracy join him. Tracy didn't actually expect that he would; it had always been so on-again, off-again. But when the Buffalo Jill had lost interest, and things kicked back up between him and Tracy in the spring, it had started to feel good, and maybe true. He was the first unmarried guy Tracy had dated in ages; the first guy with whom there was some real potential. He'd been spending a few nights a week at Tracy's place since March, up until he received this job offer.

Something about the way it had all gone down had left Tracy feeling small and sour. Perhaps it was the way he'd gleefully announced his cousin's offer without a trace of apprehension, without a single acknowledgement of the five hundred miles it would place between them. He'd called his mother right there on the spot, to share the news, and Tracy could tell from their conversation that his mother didn't even ask what it might mean for the two of them. Tracy still hadn't met the Greens.

"What about your fixer-upper?" Tracy had asked. "With a view of the lake?"

Greenie said, "Trace, we're talking Jersey. Jersey versus the Southtowns."

"I *love* the Southtowns," she said quietly, and she thought of all the times she and Greenie had shared.

"You just don't know better," Greenie said.

"That's quite a shade," Greenie said, nodding at her fingernails on her water glass.

"It's called Radioactive," Tracy said, spreading both hands out in front of her.

"It's like that slime from Nickelodeon," Greenie said. He spooned an ice cube into his mouth. "I hope Monkey does all right on the drive."

"You're taking *Monkey*?"

Greenie nodded. He'd had the orange tomcat since he was a boy and Tracy knew he was attached to the thing, but Monkey was such a *mess*, such a hassle these days. The cat was incontinent, and had to be force-fed expensive medications twice a day.

Tracy held her tongue, but fumed on the inside. She couldn't freaking believe he was taking an incontinent tomcat on that long drive and to live in his new home, and yet he hadn't even asked Tracy when she might want to visit.

When their food arrived, Greenie pointed out that the lettuce on his burger was wilted and the tomato was whitish and tough and tasteless, but he wasn't going to complain.

"See, now I've had the burgers before," Tracy said. "I told you the fish is better."

"Stuff like this won't happen at my cousin's restaurant," Greenie said.

Tracy wondered what the waitresses at Greenie's cousin's restaurant would look like. She wondered if they would all be college students. A fly cut the surface of her water and she just stared at it.

After they finished eating, Greenie said, "Do you wanna walk along the harbor? I've got a few minutes before I should hit the road."

On their way to the harbor, they passed the Naval & Military Park, where a lone attendant sat in a folding chair next to a sign that said, "$10 Tours By Request Only." The attendant wore denim shorts, a Sabres jersey, wraparound sunglasses, and a proper ship captain's hat: white with a black brim and gold piping. He held an unlit cigarette in one hand and a paperback in the other. He waved the book mildly at the two of them. An old dog at his side lifted his nose off his feet and snarled quietly.

It was a steamy Buffalo June and the air was fat with humidity. Tracy ran her finger across her damp upper lip and wiped the moisture into her shorts. A single row of geraniums lined the walkway of the harbor. The Niagara River was subdued. The air smelled of burnt seedpods and mildly of sewage. A monarch landed on her forearm and she was surprised by the tiny strong grip of its feet, before a moment later it lifted and danced away.

They walked past a boat with the words "Dale's Dream" in neat blue cursive on the side. Greenie made a terrible joke about how Dale's Dream was wet and Tracy laughed much louder and much longer than a sane person should have. They turned around at the lighthouse and didn't talk at all on their way back to the lot. The skyway zoomed in a broad, graceful arc over downtown. Tracy pulled a little cluster of sticky red Life Savers wrapped in wax paper from her pocket, and she held these in her hand for a moment, then stuffed them back in to her pocket.

When they reached his car, Greenie said, "Cool, cool, cool."

Tracy knelt to untie and retie her shoe.

A dusty trembling Plymouth Acclaim pulled up next to them and a woman lowered her window.

"Which way to the arena?" the woman shouted over a roaring commercial on her radio. "*Seven to eleven, ladies drink free*," the commercial bellowed.

"Take the overpass toward the 290," Greenie yelled, pointing. "Turn right onto Pearl. The arena's right there."

"Go Sabres!" the woman yelled.

Greenie gave her a thumbs-up and the woman drove away.

Greenie turned back toward Tracy and hugged her.

Her sadness swelled so hard and so high that she almost could have mistaken it for euphoria. He kissed her. He tasted mossy and mild and his tongue was dry.

He climbed into the car, rolled down his window, and opened the sunroof manually. Tracy's heart was screaming.

"Sayonara," Greenie said.

Tracy didn't want to go home just yet. Shelly was in town for a wedding and staying with Tracy for the weekend and Tracy knew what she would say: "He left *already*? You take the day off to spend it with him, and he leaves *before two o'clock*?"

Tracy walked slowly past the naval park again. She stared at the three sullen gray ships that loomed and groaned, stationary on the Niagara River.

The attendant was still sitting out front. Tracy got closer, and saw that he wore a sticker nametag, and *Todd* was handwritten in sloping capital letters.

Todd looked up from his book when she approached and he lifted the brim of his captain's hat half an inch with his index finger. His eyes were soggy. The sunshine on his chin illuminated a broad plum-colored bruise that spread across his jaw.

"I'd like to do the tour," she said.

"Where's yer boyfriend?"

"He's not my boyfriend."

"I thought I just seen him kissin' on you."

“Can we get started?” Tracy said.

“That’ll be ten dollars.”

She reached into her purse and pulled out a five and five ones. Todd licked his finger and thumb and counted the bills. He folded them in half and put them into the back pocket of his shorts. The dog at his feet was staring unpleasantly at Tracy, his top lip fluttering to reveal teeth.

Tracy held her open palm out in a peaceful gesture. The dog growled low.

She said, “Come on, guy,” and moved a little closer.

With unexpected agility, the old dog whipped his head out and made a move to chomp on her hand. Tracy snatched her hand back to her chest.

Todd said, “Don’t mind him, he’s got a bum leg and a tumor on his butt.”

“What’s that got to do with anything?”

“Wounded dogs,” Todd explained, “tend to get snappish. He wasn’t always this way.”

“Not much of an excuse.”

He walked Tracy down the dock a ways so they were centered in front of the sub. He spread one arm out in a wide angle behind him. “The USS *Croaker*,” he announced. The sub was massive. A yellowed flag hung motionless at the front of the thing and otherwise it was just an immense plane of dull gray with bolts and handles and hinges.

“Do you mind if I sit down?” Tracy said. She didn’t wait for his permission before lowering herself cross-legged onto the bleached and splintering wood.

“The USS *Croaker*,” Todd said again. “Three hundred eleven

feet long, fifteen hundred tons, eight torpedo tubes. They called it the *Croaker* because of the noise it cranked out. It was launched December 19, 1943."

Tracy wondered if Greenie had reached I-90 yet and what music he was listening to. She wished she had more photographs of the two of them together.

"Now this here *Croaker* was built just prior to the US entry into the World War II. My dad fought in that war. The *Croaker* was sent to the Pacific to fight against Japan's merchant marine and navy." Todd's words swam above Tracy like a fog, shapeless and peaceful and out of reach.

"This *Croaker*," he continued, "claimed eleven Japanese vessels. That included a cruiser, four tankers, two freighters, an ammunition ship, two escort craft, and a minesweeper. Am I boring you yet?"

Tracy shook her head.

"You look bored."

"*Please*, keep going," she said. "Just keep going."

THE COIN

Greenie's cousin's restaurant hadn't survived the summer. The liquor license fell through after some hang-ups with the paperwork, and they couldn't work out the kitchen ventilation system to the satisfaction of the health department. Greenie found himself suddenly jobless in August, living in central New Jersey with Monkey, his incontinent tomcat, and two thousand dollars less than he'd arrived with.

A buddy from his high school was living an hour away, in Ocean City, and when Greenie contacted him, the guy offered Greenie a temporary position with his T-shirt shop, which was located right on the boardwalk. "Only for a month or two, though," the guy warned. "Things get real quiet around here when the season changes. We'll board up and winterize the place by the end of October."

It was the second weekend of October now, meaning Greenie had ten days to find something else in order to make rent. He'd had a hard time locking down an apartment that would allow pets, but eventually he found a tolerant landlord, at the duplex he now shared with an old Chinese couple. The apartment was a few blocks off the beach, next to the boardwalk entryway with the grimy little stucco changing rooms.

To the left of his apartment was a mint-green two-story building that was advertised in elegant cursive as a "VIP Day Spa," but also included a handwritten sign out front that read in crude Sharpie, "Eggs for Sale, $2 Dozen." Greenie had never seen anyone enter the place, but he worked long days at the T-shirt shop, (he was the only employee), so he didn't know what went on at that spa when he wasn't around.

On the other side of his home was a little seafood joint, Spadafora's, with a big faded sign that read "Best Crab in OCNJ" and had a picture of a smiling pink crab in a chef's hat. The place pumped out a powerful stink of grease and fish and salt every evening during service, then they stacked up their garbage in the alleyway between the restaurant and Greenie's apartment. Sometimes, on airless nights, it became so foul and overpowering that Greenie couldn't sleep. Not that the smell inside his apartment was a whole lot better.

Monkey had been diagnosed with hyperthyroidism back in Buffalo, which explained the weight loss and shedding. Greenie had stocked up on Monkey's pricey medications before moving to New Jersey. Greenie's mother had always done most of the cat cleanup at their home, but since moving out, Greenie had become accustomed to it. He kept a box of cleaning supplies on his kitchen table for easy and immediate access upon entering the apartment; a box of latex gloves, baggies for the solid messes, carpet spray, Tilex, Febreze.

Lately, though, Monkey had taken a turn for the worse. He'd lost more weight and his coat had gone to hell. It was patchy at his joints, and lopped over his spine like an overcoat three sizes too large. Greenie had become concerned and did some research on the most affordable pet care in the area. He'd settled on a clinic called Pawscienda, located near his home. It had some good reviews on Yelp.

When Greenie dropped Monkey off at the Pawscienda that morning, he explained about the hyperthyroidism, filled out some paperwork about the cat's medical history and the medications he was currently on, and asked them to run whatever tests they'd need to. The place seemed all right. It smelled clean and plasticky, like the first day of school. The woman at the front desk had thin, shoulder-length blond hair and darkly pink-streaked cheeks. A sparkly, expensive-looking watch was buried within her fleshy wrist. She was chewing gum.

She said, "How'd you come up with the name *Monkey*?"

"I asked my folks for a monkey for my tenth birthday," Greenie said. "I got what I got."

"We all get what we get, don't we?" the woman said. "No matter what we ask for."

Greenie said he'd be back for Monkey around six.

• • •

The air was gusty and damp and the boardwalk was deserted. Greenie saw a lone surfer in a wetsuit coming in from the water. He balanced his surfboard on the top of his bald head and his bare feet slapped along the splintery two-by-fours. Greenie entered the T-shirt shop from the back entrance, then raised the chain link drop door on the boardwalk side to open the place up for business.

In the narrow but high-ceilinged T-shirt shop, three walls were covered with T-shirts, popular designs in a variety of colors and sizes. Phrases like "Shoulda Put a Ring On It" and "Ocean City Gal" and "Surf's Up." The artist's studio was a small area partitioned off at the back of the restaurant, containing spray guns and lots of extra paint canisters. The system was digitized; all Greenie had to do was enter the design choice into his computer at the front of the shop, go to the back and load the proper colors, spread the T-shirt over the canvas board, and within a minute or two the design was complete. Then he had to let the thing dry in front of a powerful fan for a few minutes, so the paint wouldn't drip. It was easy work compared to the stress and demands of a restaurant, but time crawled on these gaunt, gray days, when he'd make five or six T-shirts in the entire shift, or sometimes not a single one.

He had all too much time to worry about next month's rent and car payments, and Monkey.

The jangle of bells at the front door startled Greenie out of the ESPN skate competition he was watching on the miniature TV that rested on a stool next to the checkout counter. He looked toward the door, where an enormous figure was entering the shop. It was a woman, the largest woman Greenie guessed he'd ever seen; she had to be well over six feet, maybe even closer to seven. She carried a bag over one arm, and Greenie quickly realized it was a metal detector. She had a strong, arched lump of a nose, long black hair, a way of moving that was graceful yet not entirely human, like a wild creature that was trapped uncomfortably in human garb. She was deeply tan. Greenie saw folks with metal detectors on the beach all the time, but he reckoned he'd never seen this woman before. She would've stood out. Most of them were slow-moving white-haired men with Star Trek sunglasses and crooked pastel baseball caps. Greenie wondered where this woman was from, where she was headed, what she'd found to dig up on this beach.

She walked slowly in front of the display wall, gazing up and down and thoughtfully taking in the shirt designs. She paused for a long while in front of a neon green women's T-shirt with an American flag at the center and the word "Free" written in a classic black graffiti scrawl. She wore brown leather gloves and brown leather boots with tight-fitting jeans tucked into them, a hooded sweatshirt, a red New York Giants scarf around her neck. Greenie could see that the woman had already tracked in a fair amount of sand. Most customers did, but it bothered him less when it was girls in bikini tops. The woman removed her metal detector and propped it next to the umbrella stand near the front door.

She approached Greenie at the register. He was fingering a tiny surfboard keychain.

"How much for an XL?" Her voice was deep and soft.

"Depends," Greenie said, "on the pattern you choose. How many colors and all that."

He pushed the book of laminated design pictures toward her. She skimmed the book, at one point sticking a finger in a page to hold it. Greenie hummed quietly along to "Two Girls for Every Boy." His boss insisted that The Beach Boys play on a constant loop, all day long.

The woman reached the back of the book then pointed up at a row of white T-shirts behind and high above Greenie on the wall.

"I'll do one of them," she said. "In double XL."

Greenie had to use his chrome high-reach garment hook. He pulled it from his side and extended it, screwed it into place. He accidentally knocked the stick hard against the rack, and the shirts swooped unevenly left and right. He successfully hooked the T-shirt, and drew it down to the counter.

"How about the design?" he said.

She held out the book, returning to the page she'd already identified, and jabbed a picture with her gloved index finger. It was a picture of a cheesy pink sunset with the words, "Someone in Ocean City misses me." Greenie wanted to laugh. He wondered if the woman could read, if she intended to give it as a gift or wear it herself.

"You got it." Greenie entered the picture code into his computer, and went back to the studio to create the shirt. He watched the woman through a hinged seam in the partition. She went to the front of the shop and gazed out, across the boardwalk, to the water. Five or six shirtless little boys passed the front of the shop. They looked cold, cupping their hands together and hunching their shoulders. They all wore swim trunks and those newfangled webbed water shoes. The woman watched them pass and took a step toward the door. Only once before had someone walked out on a T-shirt while it was being made.

He finished the shirt and brought it back to the counter, hung it with yellow plastic clothespins on the line against the wall behind him, and set the fan on high directly in front of it.

"Whattya think?" he said.

"Can I wash it?" she asked.

"Only in cold," Greenie said, "and only air-dry."

After a minute or two, he took the shirt down, ran his fingers over the design, and folded it neatly. He slid it into a flat brown paper bag.

"It'll be sixteen twenty-three," he said.

The woman reached for the zippered fanny pack that swung at her groin and pulled out six or seven rolls of coins. Greenie expressed his annoyance with a little nose sigh. He counted the rolls, mostly dimes, and split into a roll of nickels to make the total balance. He deposited the coins into his register and his little machine spat out a receipt. He handed her this, as well as the shirt.

It wasn't until she'd left and he was starting to close the register when he glanced in and realized that one of the coins she'd paid with was in fact not a nickel. Greenie picked up the coin, which was the approximate size of a nickel, but lighter weight, and on the side that faced him was inscribed a wheel that filled the whole coin, with spokes. He turned it over in his palm and the other side read: "1 ride."

Greenie had only set foot in Wonderland, the amusement park at the far end of the boardwalk, once or twice. It opened in evenings and on weekends, and catered to little kids, featuring a dozen carnival rides, a mini-golf course, various food stands.

He recognized the coin as a token for the giant old Ferris wheel in Wonderland. Greenie had read about the wheel in the local paper; how it had been built in the 1920s, and still maintained the original operating system, whereby the guy who ran it collected coins from riders, rather than the red paper tickets required by all the other rides. The historic wheel was the largest structure in the park, and one of the tallest in the entire state of New Jersey; it was almost six stories high. Greenie had admired the wheel at night before and could see the upper half of it from his apartment. The spokes were covered with rainbow-colored lights, which blinked in and out from the center in bright circus patterns. Greenie held the coin warm in his palm for a moment, then shoved it into the front pocket of his jeans.

Greenie's shift officially ended at six, but he closed the shop a few minutes early that evening, since he had to pick up Monkey.

At Pawscienda, an old man with an old dog spread across his feet paged through a *Horse & Hound Magazine*. There was a box of Kleenex on the plexiglass coffee table at the center of the room. A girl in a navy Kroger polo shirt had a cream crate at her feet. She was running her thumb along the screen of her iPhone.

Greenie checked in with the receptionist.

She showed him back to a blindingly sterile operating room with framed certifications and degrees hung crookedly on the wall.

The veterinarian introduced herself as Dr. Scott, and she rose from a desk in the corner, where she was flipping through a stack of perforated papers, to shake Greenie's hand. She pulled her reading glasses from her nose, folded them, and hung them from the breast pocket of her white laboratory jacket.

Monkey was lying on the table on his side, licking the inside of his paw. He was clearly still sedated, each blink slow and uneven. Greenie felt suddenly nauseous.

Dr. Scott said, "The thyroid problems have advanced, as you guessed, with the weight loss and changes to his fur. The meds you started him on, when did you say? Four, five months ago? They're not keeping up."

She reached down to stroke Monkey down the center of his skull and Monkey dipped his chin a hair. She gently kept going at his nose with her middle knuckle, while reaching for a clipboard with her other hand. Greenie felt suddenly angry at Dr. Scott. Monkey had never liked having his face touched. Monkey's mouth was slightly open and the thin gray-pink tip of his tongue peeked through. The fur around his mouth was white.

Dr. Scott fiddled with the glasses in her pocket but didn't put them back on before squinting down at her chart. "Monkey's fifteen years old now, is that right? That's a good, long life for a cat." She set the chart back down and looked at Greenie. "Monkey's in a fair amount of discomfort now, with these problems. Blood pressure through the roof and constant dehydration."

Greenie nodded. He willed steadiness to his voice. "Are there other medicines we could try?"

Dr. Scott shook her head. "Methimazole is the best stuff out there. Now, the other option would be surgery. Remove the thyroid glands altogether. That's a big procedure for an old cat." She fingered Monkey's neck. "This is where the incisions would be made, this long, on both sides. We'd put him under."

Greenie nodded. He pictured Monkey spread out on this very table, deep under anesthesia with his paws limp and agape while Dr. Scott sliced into his neck. He pictured the blood.

"I'd just tell you up front," Dr. Scott continued, "it costs five, six hundred and there's a fair amount of risk involved. Long recovery too. More than a fair amount of risk with a cat this advanced."

The tip of Monkey's tail danced and swirled on the table.

"It's your decision, of course," Dr. Scott said delicately, gazing down at Monkey. "Like I said, fifteen years is a long life for a cat. Letting him go, at a point, is the merciful thing, do you know what I mean? It's your decision, of course."

Greenie swallowed. His heart felt like it would fall out of him. He tried very hard not to cry.

Dr. Scott turned to Greenie and looked him straight on. She palmed his shoulder and gave him a hard, meaningful squeeze. "It's hard to let go of someone you love."

Greenie smashed his eyes shut and reached blindly for Monkey's soft belly. He twirled his fingers through Monkey's fur and felt his fine ribs, those bones gracefully curled to protect his innards, thinner than chopsticks. He blinked and looked down at Monkey through wet eyes. Unlike the fur on Monkey's back, which was still the same deep gold-orange that it was when he was a kitten, his belly had turned into the palest corn-silk yellow. Greenie held his paw.

Dr. Scott walked Greenie to the receptionist, where he scheduled the appointment for the following week.

Instead of putting Monkey back in his crate for the ride home, Greenie carried the empty crate out of the office in one arm, and Monkey in the other. He held Monkey like a tired child; Monkey's front paws draped over Greenie's shoulder, head cradled to Greenie's neck, his hind legs dangling free. Monkey was soft and heavy and lumpy, like an under-stuffed down pillow, and he vibrated happily against Greenie's chest.

Where he ought to have headed west, inland, toward his apartment, Greenie decided instead to drive back toward the boardwalk. He parked in the lot behind Auntie Anne's. The lights of Wonderland were on. He pulled Monkey from where he slept on a Buffalo Bills beach towel in the backseat. He wrapped the towel around Monkey and carried him at his chest. Monkey stirred and sniffed the air and swiped once, mildly, at Greenie's neck with his paw.

Greenie entered the park from the boardwalk side. The rides were all active although there was scarcely a rider in the entire park, from what he could see. The empty carousel spun slowly and tinkled a lazy circus tune. Bumper cars hummed and moaned lazily against each other, migrating slowly in several large packs from one side of the rink to the other. Several employees gathered around the hot pretzel stand passed their smartphones to one another and chuckled at short videos. They didn't seem to notice Greenie when he passed.

Pop music crackled over the intercom and was barely audible over the rush of the water cycle that delivered log carriages up to their peak at the Log Drop ride, and sent them plummeting down the drop. Greenie watched, as one after another, empty four-passenger log carriages slowly ascended, paused and teetered briefly at the peak, then whooshed down. It was a strange thing to watch without accompanying chatter and shrieks.

Greenie made his way past the small stage where a balloon animal artist had performed the last time he'd been there. The thick mustard-colored velvet stage curtain was drawn back to reveal an empty stage with a Mountain Dew bottle on its side, and a damp-looking newspaper with a rubber band around the center. Greenie passed the guy who'd guess your weight for a dollar and give you five back if he wasn't within ten pounds. The guy was sitting in a lawn chair next to the scale, the hood of his sweatshirt up around his face, one earbud in his ear and the other dangling at his stomach. Greenie had always wondered if you could scam those guys by filling your pockets with rocks. He continued on past the cotton candy machine, where furry strips of pink clung to the inner walls of the transparent cage, and a girl stood ready with a stack of thin, white cardboard cones.

Greenie finally reached the Ferris wheel, where a long gated ramp, designed to organize a single-file line, lead up to the loading platform. There was no one in line when Greenie approached, and the platform was empty. In fact, the wheel wasn't moving at all, despite the illusion of activity by the brightly pulsing bulbs on the spokes. The kid who operated the thing was sitting on a stepladder at the base of the wheel. He wore a newsboy cap and a black bowtie over an ill-fitting collared shirt.

Greenie made his way up the ramp, approached the platform, reached into his pocket, and handed the kid his "1 ride" coin. He clutched Monkey within the towel.

The kid took the coin from Greenie's hand, but didn't drop it into the fancy old-fashioned machine with antique gold trim. He peered into the towel at Greenie's chest. He laughed. "Yo, I thought that was a baby at first. Sorry, man, no can do."

"What?"

"We can't let animals on here." The kid held out the coin to return it.

Greenie was a good six inches taller than the kid, and he glared down at him. He didn't take the coin. The kid had braces and an oily chunk of rust-colored hair across his forehead. "I need to take my cat," Greenie said. He tightened the towel against his chest. Monkey made a slow grunting rattle.

The kid said, "It's the rule, man. Surprised they even let you in the park with that thing. Usually they don't unless it's a service animal, like a blind-person dog." The kid laughed. "You've got some balls, dragging a *cat* in here like that, yo."

"This place is deserted," Greenie said. "Nobody's gonna care. Can I just go for my ride now, like I paid you for?" He nodded toward the coin in the kid's hand.

"It's gonna be my ass if they see you, man."

Greenie took a step toward the loading deck.

The kid glanced nervously over both of his own shoulders then out into the park beyond Greenie. "All right, man, just, you've gotta say if anyone says anything, say you hid him, all right? Just say you snuck him on underneath the towel or something, all right, man?"

Greenie nodded and stepped up onto the platform. The kid dropped the coin into the machine and gestured toward the empty cart before them.

Greenie held Monkey with his left arm and used his right to grasp the handlebar to steady himself while entering the cart. He took a seat facing outward, away from the center of the wheel, and set Monkey next to him. The seat was a pleasing bouncy soft plastic that squeaked beneath his thighs. The kid lowered the safety bar to rest loosely at Greenie's waist, and Greenie pulled Monkey from his side to arrange him across his lap.

He nodded at the kid. "Thanks, man."

The kid grabbed a clutch and pulled it toward him to move the wheel a few notches clockwise, so Greenie's cart lifted off the platform and ten feet into the air, where it swung gently, slightly lopsided from Greenie's weight. The kid pushed that manual clutch back into place and pressed a big illuminated green button on the raised control column at his side.

The kid leaned back against the control column as the wheel hissed and groaned into action. It accelerated faster than Greenie expected, and made him dizzy for a moment. When he reached the top of the cycle, he sucked in cool, thick air as his inner ear adjusted.

Greenie stroked Monkey's small skull. Monkey's eyes were closed and his paws worked slowly in and out against Greenie's thigh. They circled around five or six more times, and this time when they reached the bottom platform the kid caught Greenie's eye and said, "Last time around, all right, man? I'll give you a sec at the top."

On this final cycle, the wheel slowed as it approached the crest. It got slower and slower, and when his cart reached the very tip-top, the wheel groaned to a complete stop. The cart swayed. It was early dusk, and everything was suddenly so fresh and crystallized before Greenie it was like a pair of old contact lenses had been peeled away from his eyeballs. He looked out beyond the boardwalk, beyond the wide, white beach, to the ocean. The water was taupe, churning and rolling mildly, like a massive silk sheet shaken out in slow motion. There was a fire down on the beach, and a large figure stoked it with what looked like a two-by-four.

Greenie felt the gentle tickling pulse of Monkey's claws in his leg. The appointment was in five days. He wondered if, when the time came, he'd actually be able to leave his home, make that drive to Pawscienda, carry Monkey into that building, stand next to him while they did the thing.

He thought about what Dr. Scott had said: "It's hard to let go of something you love."

Love. Greenie considered this.

Love, that word no woman had ever torn from him. His thoughts veered suddenly, unexpectedly, to a memory of the worst fight he'd had with Tracy—it was the only time she had ever used that word—last winter after she had discovered that he was dating the much-younger cheerleader. Tracy was livid.

She had said, "We're together for a year and you won't even hold my hand." Greenie closed his eyes and remembered now how furiously Tracy's lips had trembled, how she'd thrown her palm in front of her mouth in a bad attempt to contain herself.

He remembered thinking that she looked very old, but she was crying a child's tears. "You're with this girl two weeks," she'd continued, in a tight, fractured voice, "and you're telling the world about it. Like it's the real deal. Like you're in *love* with her, or something."

"Who said anything about love?" Greenie had scoffed. He was all squirrelly and pissed, because Tracy had made him feel guilty now, and he didn't want to feel guilty. He didn't want to feel anything. He was pissed, so he'd gotten a little mean with her. "And so what if I am?" he said. "I can love whoever I want."

Tracy's face had broken then. She hid it inside her sweater. Greenie waited. He looked out the window. A spider traversed the sill. He followed it until it disappeared, then he looked back at Tracy.

Her voice was raw and forceful when it burst from behind her sweater: "*So can I.*"

These words were not the words Greenie had imagined pent up inside her.

It was the only time the word would come up between them, rearing its enormous and unwelcome head.

Greenie's cart swayed, but it was only the breeze—they hadn't yet moved beyond the crest of the wheel. The view really was magnificent. The herringbone pattern of the boardwalk shimmered and bent.

He'd never been in love with Tracy, not even remotely, or at least he'd convinced himself of that at the time. She was too old, and too depressing. She asked for so little. She'd never asked him to love her, and he'd never offered that he might. He'd never for one moment imagined a future with her. But as he thought about it now, it occurred to him that, strangely, something in there seemed to have nonetheless been a very real deal. There was something more than just the slapping together of bodies, the sharing of food, the passage of time spent together. Time had bleached out thoughts of all the other far-more-attractive women he'd ever been with, whereas Tracy was still as bright and clear as a spring morning in his mind.

Did he love her? This thought startled him. It didn't matter anymore, he supposed. If he did, it had never been a romantic love, but this stormy warmth he felt all through his chest . . . Had he been wrong? Was it love, after all? And if so, why was that word so slow to make its way up and out of him?

Was love perhaps much bigger, much weirder, much less voluntary than he had always expected?

Greenie smiled sadly, wondering what Tracy would make of him now; about to be broke and unemployed in this strange city where he knew no one, riding a Ferris wheel with this dying cat on his lap. She wouldn't be very sympathetic. Tracy hated cats. He wondered what she was getting into these days; what was the latest business idea she was cooking up, and if she'd sold her house. They hadn't been in touch since he'd left—not a single text or email in months. That had surprised him. He didn't think she'd let go so easy.

Greenie thought again of her voice that day when they fought, her pain. It had occurred to him in that moment that perhaps he was much more powerful than he realized. Greenie looked down now at the people on the earth below him, the scattered few Wonderland employees and beyond them, a handful of people making their way down the boardwalk, and beyond them, three or four people walking alone on the beach. It occurred to Greenie now that all these people were probably more powerful to someone than they realized. And all these people were probably powerless to someone too.

That fire down on the beach was now raging. Licking at the air above it with red tongues. It looked inviting, alive. As far as he could tell, there was still just that one person tending it.

Greenie remembered then that Tracy's birthday was in October, although he couldn't recall the exact date, and he wondered if she'd gotten those sideline tickets, like she always talked about doing for her birthday. He really, really hoped that she had. He felt the weight of Monkey, even, still, and silent across his thighs, and he waited patiently for the wheel to move on.

CALLAHAN'S

It was mid-November and Laura needed to clear her head after a day of ominous silence in her house. She hadn't yet made up her mind about the pregnancy. Jim was still in Waco, Texas. Charlie was in his room and she knocked on the locked door to ask if he wanted her to pick up anything for dinner. When he didn't answer his door, she texted his phone, and he responded, by text, that he had no appetite. Laura decided to go to the Southtowns, where she would be certain not to run into Kevin or any of his friends or coworkers.

Things with Kevin had started to go downhill last winter. He became irritable with Laura, pointing out the places where she'd gained a bit of weight and poking fun at her Southtowns accent.

He got impatient when she expressed concern over Charlie. Kevin claimed that his oldest son had gone through something like this when he was thirteen—that it was a phase and Laura didn't need to fuss so much about it. The kid was fine, Kevin said. He offered Laura brief, lackluster shoulder rubs.

Kevin's perspective on this changed one snowy evening, when Laura and Kevin returned from dinner to find Simon, Kevin's beloved hyacinth macaw, missing. Kevin was livid, and insistent that Charlie had done something horrible to the bird. He claimed he knew that Charlie had always hated Simon. Laura didn't know what to think. She listened to Charlie's story about the crazy woman who came in for help and ran away with Simon. Kevin didn't buy a word of it, even after Charlie produced her wet clothing. Kevin got the meanest he'd ever been with Charlie, calling him a weirdo, a psychopath, a bad seed. Laura tried to make peace between the two, claiming she believed Charlie's story and urging Kevin to relax and give the kid a break, but deep down, she too suspected that Charlie was lying.

Laura had a history of being lied to, but there was one major difference between being lied to by Charlie versus Jim: she had always been able to tell when Jim was lying to her. She didn't even need to see the bar tab or smell the liquor to know when he'd been somewhere he claimed he hadn't. And then, years into their marriage, when he started seeing another woman, Laura sensed it immediately. She wasn't all *that* surprised; she and Jim hadn't slept together in six months. What did she expect, really?

But the fact that Jim was incapable of lying made it all the more puzzling when he claimed (truthfully, as far as Laura could tell) that his relationship with the other woman hadn't been sexual.

"Then *what was it?*" Laura demanded.

Jim looked as stricken as a child being punished for the first time, but he had the weariness of a very old man. "It was . . . she felt . . . *safe*, I guess. Something comforting about it." His shame was palpable and stinking up the room like rot. He wouldn't meet Laura's eyes.

"Safe?" Laura screamed with a mean laughter. "*Comforting?*"

"I guess so," Jim said.

"In what way? *Tell me more*," Laura said.

Jim exhaled and looked out the kitchen window. "She doesn't know me." He poked a hole in the paper towel that he held. "Or, I guess, she doesn't know enough to be disappointed in me."

Shrill laughter escaped from Laura once again, even as tears blistered over her lids. "So she's just your '*comforting*' friend who I've never met and who you lie about seeing?"

"I wouldn't even call her a friend." Jim put his finger through the hole in the paper towel and spun it slowly, his eyes darting toward the cabinet beneath the sink, where Laura happened to know that he stashed liquor sometimes.

Laura sat down at their kitchen table. She was inclined to believe Jim only because he'd proven himself incapable of lying, but this didn't change her view that the marriage was over. The disintegration of their relationship over the past five years had been so gradual, the end so inevitable, that by now the pain was constant, dull and deeply tiresome, like terminal cancer. She could barely even muster up the energy for this fight, which ought to have been a good one.

"Do you want me to leave you?" she finally said, quietly. "Do you want to leave me?"

Jim didn't come to join her at the table. He said, "I want to deserve you." He was facing the other direction, out the window, speaking over his shoulder. Laura didn't interject to reassure him that he deserved her.

She mulled silently, bitterly, over his words, long after they'd been spoken. *Too good for him, just like he always said? He doesn't deserve me, and one day I'll realize it too? Well, fine*, she thought. *If he's so convinced of that that he's willing to let it ruin him, he might as well spend the rest of his life believing it's true.*

Jim wasn't a bad man—Laura was still convinced of this—but was he a great man? Was he even a good man? Had he ever been? How could a good man be consumed with such black and crippling self-doubt? How could a good man refuse to believe that *one good thing* existed about him, how could a good man so persistently refuse to be loved? For too many years, Laura had puzzled over why she was unable to make Jim happy. She had wasted too much time trying to improve herself in attempts to recapture their early love. In her failure to do this, her failure to save Jim from the dark sadness that had overtaken him, Laura had become cold and resilient and smug. Could a good man bring out such an ugly side of her?

It wasn't the fact that Jim didn't have a high school diploma, drank too much, and had crowded front teeth that overlapped one another. It wasn't these or any of the other things Laura knew that Jim hated about himself. It wasn't even this other woman, whatever their relationship had or hadn't been, that caused Laura to accept defeat. It was the darkness that had saturated their life together and went deeper than the sum of all these things. Laura didn't know where it began and she didn't believe it could ever be extinguished.

Laura asked Jim to start packing up his things and she said there was no big rush.

Rain beat the windows of Callahan's. Laura sat at the bar. She ordered a Sprite and a basket of onion rings from the bartender, and watched *Wheel of Fortune* on mute.

A woman eased into the barstool next to Laura. The woman was very tall and broad-shouldered, a gambler-style cowboy hat shadowing her face. Laura was mildly annoyed that the woman had chosen the seat right next to hers, when there were several other empties, but she was intrigued by the woman's size and her garb—she was dressed in thick flannels and denim and worn leather, like a lumberjack. She pulled off a pair of brown leather gloves and slapped them onto the bar before her.

When the bartender made her way over, the woman ordered chicken tenders and a coffee.

Laura said, "Good choice." She squeezed a slice of lime into her Sprite.

The woman said, "Never been here before, just took a guess."

Laura said, "My memory is that the fried stuff is good, you wanna stay away from the chowder. And the tacos, if they still do those. I used to come a lot, but only been here once or twice in the past ten years."

The woman removed her hat and set it on the bar. She smoothed her long hair back from her face, which was aged, masculine, beautiful. "You leave the area?"

"Sort of," Laura said. "Still have a soft spot for this place, though. Spent a few good nights here."

"That why you came back tonight?"

"Nah," Laura said. "Just in the mood for onion rings, and I didn't feel like putting on decent clothes to go downtown."

Laura was quiet for a while. She saw a woman at the far end of the bar and thought for a moment that it was her friend Sally, who she hadn't spoken to since high school. They were friends on Facebook, and this is how Laura happened to know that Sally had a five-year-old girl named Chloe who had some condition—in all of her pictures she had tubes coming out of her nose. Sally's husband posted inspirational sayings and links to research on Chloe's condition. Sally wore her hair the same way she had in high school—big bangs, badly contrasting highlights. This woman at the bar, Laura quickly realized, was not Sally but easily could have been, or any of the other women whose friendship had been lost in the years. Laura wondered what these women must think of her; if Sally wondered why, with that house and all the fancy vacations, Laura had not contributed to the online fund for Chloe's care.

Laura's onion rings arrived, with a little cup of ketchup. She picked one up and it was too hot, so she put it back and licked her fingers.

She thought of the first night she and Jim kissed, all those years ago, at this very bar. They were just a couple of kids! So healthy, so hopeful. It was snowing—around Christmastime. She remembered the heat that raced through her young blood that night. It was flurrying dreamily outside, and colorful big-bulbed lights were strung up along these ceiling beams. There was a massive fake spruce in the corner, covered in cheap metallic balls, tinsel, empty Jell-O shot containers and cocktail napkins with crude drawings. Christmas music bellowed, and bar guests shouted along, out of tune and behind the beat, arms around shoulders, bleary eyes and big smiles, looking to meet someone new or impress someone old. The bartender was a heavyset girl in a spandex elf suit. Sally danced lewdly with a life-size cardboard Santa, and men roared. Laura had been too quickly outpaced by her friends that night, and found herself unpleasantly sober. Jim seemed to be in the same boat.

"Having fun?" she had said.

"I guess," he said.

"Me too," she said, and they both stared out into the bar full of people having fun.

Later that night, when Jim kissed her, he held her head like it was a tiny and expensive thing, and she felt music zoom through her.

Now, Laura turned to the woman next to her. "You might be right."

The woman had her chicken and she finished chewing before asking, "'Scuse me?"

Laura said, "Right that something in me wanted to come back to a place that was good to me once. You ever done that?"

The woman tore apart a piece of chicken, which released a puff of steam. "Sure," she said, as though she hadn't necessarily been impressed with the results.

"What'd you find there?" Laura said.

"I found it was impossible to locate the same exact place."

Laura used her straw to poke at the lime in her Sprite and she took a sip. "How so?"

"The way the world works . . ." the woman explained, "the way it moves as a planet, always shiftin' and rumblin' deep inside . . . turns out no place is ever quite the same as it was before. Landmarks and coordinates will've changed."

"Oh, you're getting all scientific about it."

"Well . . ." The woman blew on a piece of chicken to cool it. "I just found that things are always shifting a few millimeters this way or that way, sittin' a little bit different on this earth every time you return to them." She popped the chicken into her mouth.

Laura thought of the last night she had spent here, also with Jim, just two months earlier; the night she became pregnant. Jim had moved back to the area a while ago, but they had not spoken. Desperate and alone, Laura had finally caved and called him. The tension between Charlie and Kevin had put her over the edge and she was on three different anxiety medications. She had also discovered that Kevin was having an affair, but this was the least of her concerns. She told Jim everything about Charlie; the disappearance of the bird, the weird stuff on his Internet browsing history, the worrisome things he'd said to classmates, the school's recommendation that he receive professional help. She had essentially stopped sleeping and resorted to distractions, losing herself to the Internet for many hours every night, researching mental health and celebrity gossip and weight loss products until dawn.

Jim let her talk and talk that night, and when he finally spoke, his voice at the other end of the line was gentle and eager. He sounded like an old, dear friend.

They had arranged to meet here at Callahan's. Laura hadn't set foot in the place since their split. Laura ordered fish and chips and Labatt Blues. Jim had a Reuben sandwich and coffee. He said he was almost two years sober. He was living a few blocks away, in the second story of a townhouse he shared with two graduate students at Buff State. They finished their meal and went to his home. He didn't even have air conditioning, just a fan in every window. He peered into his refrigerator and offered her an O'Doul's. He apologized that he didn't have anything better.

When she touched him, he wept.

Laura hadn't used protection for years; Kevin had had a vasectomy before they met. And she was in her thirties, for heaven's sake, these things only happened to kids, didn't they?

She hadn't thought much of her first missed period, as her cycle always got weird when her weight fluctuated. But after the second missed period and the onset of nausea, she went to the doctor and it was confirmed. She was already six weeks along. She called Jim, who was in Waco at the time, on a month-long assignment, and he offered to come home right away. She said that wouldn't be necessary—that she wanted to research her options first. She didn't tell another soul. She researched her options.

The woman had finished her meal and was paying in cash.

Laura used her fork to peel back the breading of her onion ring, exposing a shrimpy little something that was not really a slice of onion but merely the limp shred of its skin. "These are not actually very good," she said, mostly to herself.

TALL TALES

It was the twenty-fourth of December. Tracy had just dropped off a few bags at the Salvation Army then stopped in at Wegman's to pick up a jug of eggnog and a log of premade snickerdoodle dough. She'd wrap gifts tonight, and drive up to Shelly's house tomorrow morning.

On her way home, Tracy got off Route 5 to cruise down Baynard Street. She had been passing the Greens' house every time she was out and about for several weeks now, curious to know if Greenie would be home for the holidays. It would be very unlike him not to spend Christmas at his mother's, even if things were busy at his cousin's restaurant in New Jersey. But she hadn't seen any sign of Greenie. Not his Honda, nor any unfamiliar vehicle with Jersey plates parked out front of his parents' home, and nothing but darkness in his second-floor bedroom. Not that she would pay him a visit or give him a call or anything if his car *did* show up; she'd just want to know, was all.

It was 5:00 p.m. and after a day of steady snowfall, the streets were packed hard and slick.

Upon reaching the Greens' home, Tracy was startled to see Greenie's parents out front of the house, stringing lights up just below the gutter. The front of their little yellow house was dusted with snow. The big wreath on their front door was crooked; the velvety red bow hung loose. Tracy slowed her truck inconspicuously to a complete stop. Their house sat out near the road, and Tracy's truck wasn't more than twenty, thirty feet now from Greenie's parents. She kept her truck in gear.

Tracy had only caught a few faraway glimpses of Greenie's father over the years, and never his mother in person. His father was at the top of a stepladder with a drooping fistful of big-bulbed multicolored Christmas lights in one hand and a cable stapler in the other. Greenie's mother was at the base of the ladder, feeding him lengths of the lights. Tracy thought it very curious to be putting up lights on Christmas Eve.

Greenie's mother was overweight. Tracy had only seen her in photographs where she was wearing makeup and had her hair done up big and nice. Here now she looked so plump and plain and slow-moving in her knee-high snow boots over sweatpants, a puffy teal coat, and red knit cap. As Greenie's mother passed the lights upward to her husband, she took a moment with every single bulb, to double check that it was screwed tightly into its socket. Tracy stared at Mrs. Green's round pink face. She was very focused on the task at hand. She wore a little smile that twitched and flickered like a drowning flame.

A familiar feeling crawled from Tracy's stomach up to her throat and it rested there, thick and wet. She thought of all the times Greenie had backed out of important things or simply not shown up. How she'd felt each time, receiving the news that he wasn't coming to such and such after all, or she was disinvited from such and such; that fierce and helpless reality that she couldn't make him want her as much as she wanted him.

Then, without meaning to, Tracy thought back further, *much* further, to the first times she'd had this same feeling, when she was a kid; long before she knew Greenie. Back when she'd waited on phone calls from her dad, begged him for fishing trips, all the times he hadn't followed through. Sure, he phoned sometimes, and took her out fishing when he was around, but not near as much as she'd have liked. She could never count on him the way you want to count on a person. She thought about that forty-pound tiger muskie her dad was always talking about. How, supposedly, the thing lived in some taxidermy office up in Wawa, Ontario, but for as proud as he'd been, he didn't have any photographs, and hadn't ever had the wherewithal to retrieve the thing, in all those years. She was pretty sure it had been a tall tale all along. All these men, with all their tall tales.

Tracy put her truck in gear. She chewed on a Good & Plenty she had found on the passenger seat. She watched Mrs. Green pause on an unlit bulb and shake it next to her ear. She flicked it with her finger, re-screwed the bulb into its socket, and it lit up orange. Greenie's mother had always sounded like such a nice lady. What on earth could he be doing on Christmas Eve that was so important he couldn't come home to his mother? *Jesus Christ.* Tracy was mad now. She was glad she hadn't called Greenie once in the last six months, sent any texts, or attempted friendship on Facebook. She didn't miss 99 percent of him.

She wondered if Mrs. Green had bought him presents already, if they were wrapped and under a tree inside. Once, when they were together, Greenie had mentioned that what he really wanted for Christmas was one of the old Aud seats. The city of Buffalo had demolished the auditorium years earlier, and the Sabres' home was relocated to the nearby HSBC Arena. The lot was yet to be cleaned up, now an asbestos-infested eyesore just off the canal. They were still trying to make a buck off it, though, selling the old seats from the Aud as keepsakes. They weren't cheap either, two or three hundred apiece. But Greenie had attended Sabres games there as a kid, with his dad, and he was nostalgic for the place. At the time Greenie left for New Jersey, Tracy was actually saving up to get one of those seats for him. What a crock.

A little dog bounced in the snow in the next lawn over, and a snowplow approached in Tracy's rearview mirror. A chickadee flew in a low circle over the Greens' Rubbermaid mailbox. She wondered what percentage of *her* Greenie missed, if any.

She looked back at his parents one more time. Mrs. Green said something to her husband and he reached down to sweetly pat her little red cap.

THE
CALLER

Tracy was up at 5:00 a.m. on Christmas morning, startled by a dream. She lay still for a moment, the details still echoing inside of her. A set of teeth within her mouth that, when her tongue met them from behind, did not resemble hers. A man's shoe in her left hand, or perhaps it was a deflated football, and the sudden awareness that she was underwater, although this did not seem to pose any immediate challenges. She was wide-awake now, edgy and vigilant, rattled too far from sleep, so she got out of bed.

Her kitchen floor was very cold. The fluorescent light snapped on with its familiar reluctant twitter, and a sizable roach dissolved into the baseboard on the far wall. She stuffed an oversized bagel into her toaster, discarded the filter caked with yesterday's damp grounds from her single-serve Coffee-mate, and started a fresh pot. The family meal at Shelly's wasn't until two o'clock, but she figured she'd head up to their place early so she could take that snowy drive nice and slow, and be there hours before the meal to distribute her gifts and help out in the kitchen.

Tracy noticed a new bubble in the linoleum floor. She pressed her toe into it and the bubble changed shape then split in two. Her realtor had recommended that she have this flooring replaced before putting the house on the market, but Tracy hadn't thought it necessary. The home had been on the market for several months now, and a middle-aged lesbian couple was showing some interest. It was a little weird, Tracy thought, what her mother would've said about that and all, but she figured this was just fine. Times were changing. She had briefly crossed paths with the couple during the first showing and wondered if they found her attractive. The couple hadn't yet made an offer, but her realtor kept saying he thought they were close. Tracy had decided to move forward with the sorting and packing of her things in order to make way for the lesbians, so the workload would be less when the sale actually happened. Besides, the little pink ranch house down the street that she had her eye on wouldn't hold half the stuff she owned now. Just the day before, she had made a trip to the Salvation Army to drop off several bags of old *Redbook* magazines, some throw pillows, a Crock-Pot with a tenacious crust of orange across the bottom.

Tracy spooned a pile of black seeds into the little tray attached to the side of her hyacinth macaw's cage. The bird opened his dumb gold-rimmed eyes and shrugged his cobalt blue wings. He snapped his beak and dipped his head like he was getting ready to say something, and Tracy said, "Shut it, Simon." She was tired of that bird.

She found her warped reflection in the toaster and examined the early suggestion of a pimple near her lip. Tracy estimated that her face was just shy of *very pretty*, anymore, with one eyebrow arched higher than the other and skin that had seen too much sun and too many cigarettes, but she had lovely eyes, so dark and deep that someone had once compared them to shotgun barrels, and she had a great body for her age; men at bars said so all the time.

She poured coffee into her Buffalo Bills mug, then added a splash of York Peppermint Pattie creamer, which she'd stolen from her workplace. No one else there was drinking it anyway—all the kitchen guys took their coffee black. She blew into her coffee to distribute the cream and removed her bagel from the toaster. She spread margarine across both halves and ate over her kitchen sink. Romeo, the calico tomcat that lived in the Harts' house, sat in their darkened bathroom windowsill and pawed at the drawstring of the half-open blinds until he noticed Tracy across the way, then he just stared. Tracy made a violent gesture at him. She hated cats. Romeo stared at her a bit longer, then returned to his drawstring. The Harts' home stood in the way of Tracy's view of the water, even from her second floor. She couldn't be sure without setting foot in the little pink ranch home, but by her estimation, a sliver of lake would be visible between its neighbors to the west.

After finishing her breakfast, Tracy dragged the stack of wrapped Christmas gifts for Shelly's family into her kitchen, where she piled them high next to the door so she wouldn't accidentally leave any behind. She could hardly wait to see Shelly's face when her family opened up these gifts: for Kristen, a pink iPod mini with her name bedazzled on it; for Jay, a motorized

Tonka truck with turn signals and a horn. A juicer for Shelly, and a Kenneth Cole wallet for Shelly's husband, Mac.

In years past, Tracy had given her niece and nephew weird little assortments of cheap office supplies, rubber coin purses stamped with the name of a local car dealership, plastic-wrapped snacks from the 7-Eleven on the drive up. Shelly was going to be flabbergasted at the amount of money Tracy had spent this year. Shelly had no idea Tracy had that kind of money. Tracy hadn't gotten squat in the way of an inheritance from either of her parents, nor had she seen a dime for the house yet. No, this money had come unexpectedly, from a man named Bruce Lemon who lived in Paxico, Kansas, population: 224. Tracy had managed to keep the money a secret since a few weeks prior, when it had all gone down.

Planning for the holidays, Tracy had decided to sell a pair or two of the earrings she'd made with her father's lures on eBay. She thought she might get a little cash and at the very least some context for pricing and feedback from buyers. She threw one of the shabbier pairs of earrings, some little yellow mayfly lures with chintzy-looking heart-shaped gold charms, up on the site, and listed the minimum price as eight dollars. Not more than an hour or two later, there were multiple interested buyers, and a bidding war began. One buyer contacted Tracy to ask if the gold was real. She answered honestly that she didn't know, but doubted it. The price of the earrings inched up over the course of the week, then soared in the final minutes. A buyer named Bruce Lemon won in the end, purchasing the earrings for fifty-eight dollars.

When she contacted this Lemon guy for shipping info, he explained that he owned a little boutique in Paxico, Kansas. His boutique was the only place of its kind for miles and miles. It's where all the local gals came for new fashions. Tracy mentioned that the earrings were part of an entire line—that she had dozens more already made, and also a few articles of clothing. Lemon asked to see photographs of the other items, and pricing info. Tracy emailed this to him.

Bruce Lemon wrote back within the hour, offering outright to buy the entire collection. Even the earrings made from wax worms! He was stocking up in advance for the holiday season. He loved Tracy's style and her eye for detail, and he thought it was just right for the ladies of Paxico. He was particularly impressed by her handiwork, and Tracy did not mention that her father had done the bulk of it. Tracy decided to drive a hard bargain, and said she'd think it over, that it would take her a while to replenish her stock, and if she wasn't able to do so by January, La-Di-Da, the local boutique to which she had promised lots of merchandise, would be disappointed when she didn't have enough items to fill her shelf after all. Bruce Lemon got back to her right away with an even higher offer.

Tracy quickly decided she couldn't refuse Bruce Lemon's offer, especially with the holidays only weeks away. Bruce Lemon transferred her the money through PayPal, and extra to cover the cost of expediting the shipping. The money was in her account by noon the next day.

Bruce Lemon emailed Tracy a thank-you after his items had arrived, and he said she *must* visit his boutique if she was ever passing through. Tracy Googled his name and the town of Paxico, Kansas, population: 224. Lemon's little business didn't have a website, but then again neither did hers.

Tracy could hardly wait to tell Shelly this story while the two of them drank flavored vodka sodas and complimented changes to one another's appearance.

Tracy hadn't done much in the way of decorations in her own home this year, just a little garland over the fireplace, a tiny stand-up tree next to her flat-screen, a reindeer hand towel in the kitchen. Looking now at the bare spot in her living room, where a full-size tree ought to have gone, she thought of the lesbians. She wondered if they celebrated Christmas, and what kind of decorations they might put up in this house. She tried to picture them waking together this Christmas morning, in the same bed and everything, out in their current home in Tonawanda. Exchanging presents with each other, maybe having a lunch with their extended families if the families were accepting of all that stuff.

Tracy shivered into her coffee and looked out her window, beyond the Harts' covered pool and garage where their silver flagpole was irradiated by the light of the full moon, and the flag billowed in slow motion. She felt a swift pang of uneasiness, the sense of something left undone, an apology she owed, RSVP she'd neglected to return, a bill left unpaid, but she was unable to name the source of this feeling.

Her thoughts were pierced by the harsh jangle of the old rotary phone hanging next to her on the kitchen wall, above her Buffalo Sabres calendar. Her mother had insisted on keeping the landline although they'd both had cells for years, and even after her mother had passed, Tracy hadn't bothered to disconnect it.

The service was free with her Internet connection, and folks said it was smart to have on hand for emergencies and so forth. But now she couldn't remember the last time that phone had rang. She wondered if her mother was still listed in the phone book.

She stared at the ringing phone, the hard sepia-colored plastic, the small transparent ring of numbers vibrating gently with each ring. The cord hung in a knotty, lopsided coil. Between each ring, her ears screamed with silence.

Five o'clock on Christmas morning? What on earth . . . Tracy snatched up the receiver and put it to her ear.

She felt a human at the other end of the line, but that was all. The caller didn't speak. She smashed the phone tight to her ear for any clues; male or female, young or old. An embarrassed caller who'd dialed a wrong number. But the caller didn't breathe audibly and didn't hang up.

Tracy said, "Hello?"

She wasn't superstitious, nor easily spooked, but she felt something cold and icky and unfriendly in the thrum of silence at the other end of the line.

She slammed the phone back into its receiver and stared at it for a moment. She knelt to retie the stiff leather laces on her little moccasin slippers. The side sewing was all twisted and fraying—these slippers hadn't been the same since she'd thrown them in with the laundry. She stood, and her heartbeat thrashed her eardrums. She waited for the phone to ring again, and a moment later, it did. The Buffalo Bills bobblehead doll on her windowsill nodded at her.

THE CALL

It was very early Christmas morning, five o'clock or so, when Charlie found the phone number. He had been woken by his mother's phone call; they were boarding the plane in Atlanta after the second flight delay and missed connection (they were initially scheduled to get back on the twenty-third). They had one more layover, but would be home by noon at the very latest, she said. They would do presents, then the big Christmas dinner with Grandma and Kevin's side of the family at five o'clock. Charlie said, "I'm not going to be hungry anyway."

"I'm sorry, Charlie," his mother said, and it sounded as though she did mean it. "You can open one of your presents now, if you want, then why don't you go back to bed and get some sleep."

Her voice sounded very tired.

Charlie went downstairs and stared at the tree. Dozens of presents wrapped beneath it, over half of them marked with his name. There was also an envelope that had arrived from his father several days earlier. When Charlie received it, he'd tossed it there on top of the presents. His father never sent money, always just a cheapo generic card with *Love, Dad* scrawled largely beneath the holiday message, like he'd spent all of ten seconds and ninety-nine cents on the thing at CVS. The envelope was cream-colored and the stamp had a Christmas wreath on it. Charlie tossed it back on the pile, then he stepped backward, raised both of his middle fingers, and swung them in a wide, directive arc in front of the pile of gifts. He didn't want anything in there. None of this was worth anything to him.

He went to his mother's study to retrieve an old video to watch. He poked around the room a bit, and caught sight of a box in the corner of the room that he hadn't noticed before. He went to the box and found that it held a stack of her old daily planners, all of them bound in Vera Bradley paisley. He had a sudden warm memory of these books, which she'd since abandoned in favor of a Blackberry and then an iPhone. He remembered how she'd pull them from her purse at the dentist's office to schedule the follow-up, or to point out that Grandma's birthday was tomorrow and they ought to pick out a cake.

Charlie sat at his mother's desk now and leafed through a few of the old planners. It contained boring stuff, mostly—hair appointments, grocery lists, exercise routines. He rifled through the stack of books to locate the one from 2003, and paged through to the approximate time that his parents had split, which was spring of that year.

Here, on the day of March 3, he found a torn and yellowy slip of paper scotch-taped to the page. Handwritten on this paper was a local phone number, in his father's handwriting. Charlie carefully peeled the tape from the paper so he could examine both sides. On the backside was faded purplish typewritten lettering that read 7 *Labatt Blue—$16.50*, and had a line for a signature, which was unsigned. A bar tab.

Charlie stared at the paper. He put it to his nose.

He lifted his mother's wireless office phone from its receiver, and it blinked green at him, fully charged. He dialed the number.

It rang seven times. He thought it strange that a voicemail hadn't yet intercepted the call and wondered if perhaps it wasn't a cell phone, or if the number was no longer in service.

He had pulled the phone from his ear and was drawing up his left index finger to end the call, when someone picked up at the other end.

Charlie pulled the phone back to his ear and pressed it tight there.

It was silent for a moment, then a woman's rough voice said, "Hello?"

Charlie didn't speak. He was shaking from his stomach.

She hung up before saying hello a second time.

He knew he had to try again—to say something this time. He knew he was close to something important. He settled himself in the chair and breathed slowly to calm his loud heart.

This time, when he dialed, it only rang once before she picked up, and he detected both fear and exasperation in her voice when she said, "Hello?"

"Hello," Charlie said.

It was quiet for a moment, then she said, "Who is this?" Her voice was laced with cigarettes.

Charlie said, "I want to know what you did to my family, in March of 2003."

"Excuse me?"

"My dad wrote down your phone number in March of 2003," Charlie said. "My mom kicked him out the next month and she saved your number for ten years. I want to know what you did. If it's your fault."

There was a moment of silence at the other end, then the voice said, "You've got the wrong person. Don't call me again."

"*Wait*!" Charlie said. He felt his voice go suddenly frantic, young sounding. He cleared his throat. "Wait. *Don't hang up*, please. I just want to know. Jim McNamara. Six foot tall. Would've been in car sales at the time. The number's written on a receipt, a bar tab with half a dozen beers on it. Like you met at a bar."

The line was silent again, and Charlie waited. He thought he heard a tiny gasp at the other end, a recognition, a memory.

"Is it you?" he said.

"Geez oh Pete, kid, it's Christmas Day," the woman said. She had a strong Southtowns accent. "Ten years is a hell of a long time."

Charlie gave her a moment to continue, and when she didn't he said, "Would you tell me what happened?"

"You know . . ." the woman started in and then paused. "Well, what the shit, I guess. You know, it was the *strangest* thing," she said.

Charlie sensed her preparing the next words, marveling over the strangeness of them before she even spoke.

"He did take my number, at a bar. And he did come to my house, number of times. And I knew he was married. It was all wrong from the get-go, I knew that. And I knew it would blow up. But you know, the strange thing, and I can swear this on my life, is that we never did anything. In *fact*, he never even kissed me." She paused. "Hey, kid, how old are you anyway? You really wanna know all this?"

Charlie said, "I'm fifteen."

"Listen," the woman said. "I don't really have a leg to stand on here, getting involved with him in the first place, and you've got no reason to take my word, but I'm telling you . . . It was the strangest thing . . ." Her voice trailed off for a moment. "What happened."

"*What happened*?"

"What happened is that he'd call me up and talk all big, all the things he wanted to do, and then he'd come over and he'd just lay down in my bed, get under the covers, and he'd sleep. *Strangest* thing. Sometimes just a few minutes, sometimes an hour or two. I'd lay next to him and read or watch TV or something. Sometimes we'd talk for a little bit, but once he was there, he'd never make a move on me, and to be honest he'd get sorta peeved if I tried to do anything. Strangest thing, how he'd just lay there and sleep. With his mouth sagged open and snoring up a storm, like it was the deepest sleep of his life."

"Why would he do that?" Charlie said. He was trying to stay calm. He knew that if he lost his temper or called her a liar, she'd just hang up and likely never take his call again.

"That's what I wanted to know too," she said. "And he said . . . isn't that funny. I haven't thought back on this in ages. He said because he was *tired*."

"*Tired*?"

"I was so puzzled by it at first," the woman said. "Didn't know if I ought to be offended, or worried he was planning to steal my stuff or chop me up and put me in a freezer or something, so after a few times, I ask him what on earth his intentions were. And he says he can't sleep at home. I'm like, so you meet a woman at a bar and use her for her bed? For naptime? What kind of a person *does* that?"

"*What did he say*?" Charlie cried. He had the receiver smashed to his ear hole. He didn't want to miss a word. "*What did he say*?" he said again.

"I finally get this much out of him—he says he can't sleep at home because he knows he's no good. Not as good as his wife deserves, anyway. Not the kind of father his kid deserves. Says he's on edge all the time, every second of the day and night, because he knows he's not good enough for his family and it's only a matter of time til his wife leaves him. Says he's a shit husband and hasn't really done nothing for himself, never gonna make much money or lose the weight, that it's only a matter of time til she's gone. So of course I'm like, 'You're out of your mind! What are you doing over here at another woman's house, giving your wife a *reason* to leave you when that's what's got you so paranoid you're losing sleep over it in the first place?' You know? It made me mad, but I also felt bad for the guy. I'm like, 'You're so tired, why don't you sleep in your car? Or a hotel?'"

"*What did he say*?" said Charlie.

"He says because he can't sleep when he's alone." She was quiet for a moment. "Awful dreams, or something. I finally gathered that the guy was just real lonely. Had a lot of stuff swimming around in his head. Negative stuff . . ."

Charlie was quiet.

"Had too much swimming around up there and didn't know what to do, but to climb into a stranger's life and make himself at home there for a little while."

Charlie couldn't speak. His eyes were closed. He felt a frightening powerful sadness climbing inside him. Charlie was picturing his dumb old dad—that dumb old face that he barely even knew anymore. He was picturing that face saying these things. That face feeling these things.

He wondered what his father was doing for Christmas. Jim had left Charlie a voicemail several days earlier, asking if Charlie wanted to spend any time together on Christmas day, but Charlie hadn't returned the call.

It was silent for a long while.

"For what it's worth," the woman finally said, "and I don't know if it's what you want to hear, but your dad didn't seem like a bad guy to me."

Charlie hung up the phone before erupting with a sob that sounded to his own ears like a huge gaping hole being ripped into the middle of a living thing.

CRUISING ALTITUDE

Laura pressed her forehead to the window of the airplane. Kevin was fast asleep beneath the fleecy airline throw blanket and his sleep mask. The flight attendants wore Santa hats and offered gingerbread snowmen for snacks. They seemed unfazed by the snow in the forecast. Laura absently reached into the pocket of her sweater and recovered a voucher for a free Pilates session with Duffy, one of the personal trainers at her gym. They had given Laura a handful of these when she renewed her membership, but she hadn't set foot in the gym in months. Laura shoved the voucher back in her pocket and ran her fingers over her stomach, swallowing back a swell of nausea. She flipped through the airline brochure from the seat pocket in front of her. It contained an index of flight terms, trivia, and explanations. It said that at cruising altitude a jet reached a speed of six hundred miles an hour. Laura gazed out the window. The sky was still dark and the airplane seemed to be resting on the bed of clouds beneath them. She could hardly believe the thing was moving at that speed. In fact, she could hardly believe it was moving at all.

She would tell Kevin after the holidays. She was thirteen weeks now, so it would soon be very obvious anyway. Laura wondered if the new baby would be a boy or girl. She remembered now that not long after Charlie had been born, Jim was ready for another. He had always wanted a daughter.

Laura closed her eyes and considered the things she knew, the things that were certain in this moment: the weight of her own head on her own neck, the warmth of the muscles inside her, the length of each breath. In this moment, it felt to Laura as though these things were truly the only certainties in her life, and they comforted her.

Then, from here, she started to consider the things that she didn't know, the things that were not certain. The particulars of a divorce. The future of her family, and that little pocket of pale fluid inside of her. She considered the way that her love for Jim had shifted and morphed over the years; the landmarks, exact coordinates, and size of this love changing every single day. She considered the fact that the next love they might share would barely even resemble their first love of fifteen years ago. And yet, something inside her suggested that even though this love would continue to change, even though it would sit a little bit differently on this earth from here on out and she could not be certain of its final destination, *even so*, this tired, sore, graceful old thing *was love*, and surely this was worth returning to.

The flight attendant came on and announced that they had reached cruising altitude. Laura looked out the window. The sky up above was still deep blue and winking with constellations, but over the horizon of thick, white cloud cover, there was gold in the distance, and soon the sun would rise and swell above the clouds.

The following month, Laura and Charlie would go to live with Jim in his second-floor apartment in the Southtowns. There was a fidelity clause in the prenuptial agreement with Kevin, and Laura would get nothing. Charlie would transfer back to public school and Laura would sell her jewelry, and some of the valuable scarves and articles of clothing, on eBay. She would get a job once the baby was born. She would learn the bus schedules.

Laura would never return to that cathedral that she so loved in Spain, or the pristine beaches of Antigua. She would never again drink a bottle of Cabernet Franc from the '70s, or eat dinner at Alouette. She would never get to visit the Ryōan-ji gardens and see the little gray-haired gardener in his silk kimono. But, she thought, it was nice to know that those gardens would still be there, and perhaps even that same little gardener, even if she couldn't see them for herself.

RED MOON

Tracy put the phone back in its receiver and stared at it for a moment. She really hoped that kid was going to be all right.

She hadn't thought about Jim McNamara in ages. She had tucked him back into that faraway part of her memory reserved for the guilt, the disappointments, the humiliations. She considered now what might've happened to that family in the time since her involvement with him. Was this her fault? The hollow heartache in that boy's voice—had she been part of that? She let herself feel this for a moment.

Tracy decided to go outside for a smoke, and maybe a little walk too. She desperately needed to get out of the house, release some of these troubles into the early morning air. It was Christmas Day, after all. Besides, it always helped clear her head to walk these streets in the strange morning hours. She pulled on her boots, winter coat, gloves.

It was terribly cold outside so she lit a cigarette then got to walking briskly to warm her muscles. She felt rotten. She couldn't get the pain of that caller's voice out of her head. All these years of thinking she deserved a better life than the one she was given, all these years of blaming the people around her . . . Now, as she considered how thoughtlessly she'd set things in motion all those years ago . . . *And there could be more*, she thought; Jim was only one of a dozen married men she'd messed around with. Something ugly inside of her had always been driven to prove that she was as good as a woman who someone considered *marriage material*—that she was every bit as desirable. There were two truths here, it occurred to her. There was the one that she could easily tell to anyone who'd listen; the one that justified her behavior, quickly wiped away the wrongdoing. And beneath that truth, attached to its underbelly, was the cruelty of carelessness, the damage left in its wake.

She threw her cigarette butt into the snow and walked in the direction of the lake, past the Harts' home and the Sullivans' garage. There were no other signs of life on the streets or in the neighborhood homes. She reached the little public-access beach a block or two later, and this is when she noticed a figure out on the lake. A good ways out; a quarter mile or so. It had been a cold winter and Erie had frozen over early, back in November, so now was fit to walk on. The full moon illuminated the faraway figure, across the glaze of frozen snow. Tracy wished she had her binoculars. She wondered what someone was doing that far out on the ice at this time of night; if perhaps they were out to take pictures of the wintry nighttime skyline, or shoveling for hockey in the morning, or just wandering.

Tracy stepped over the crumbling seawall and crossed the narrow snow-covered beach. She approached the water's edge. She was in her wedge-heeled boots, which weren't ideal for a trek through snow and across ice. When she stepped out onto the ice, no give or crackle or groan rose from beneath her, so she started out across the lake. Unable to make out what the figure was doing and if they had noticed her, she thought it best to wave in a friendly manner every few steps. The full moon lit her path.

A very large man sat on an upside-down five-gallon bucket. He looked Native American. She guessed he was from the Seneca reservation just a few miles north, near Niagara. He wore a brown knit cap and many layers of clothing. He had a beautiful face with deep, sad, strong lines, a gambler-style cowboy hat, and a long black braid that reached two feet straight and thick down his back. The bucket looked tiny beneath him—he was as big as a bear. He seemed neither startled nor irritated by Tracy's presence as she approached.

He was positioned over a hole in the ice, eight or ten inches across, and he bounced a fishing rod gently above the hole. A duffel bag sat at his side. One bloody fish lay across the ice next to his bucket. It was a good-sized fish, well over a foot long, nice and fatty in the middle. It had a spiny dorsal fin, which was still erect and shone iridescent against the ice. Its belly was gray, its wide, down-turned mouth bloody and ajar.

"Hola," Tracy said. She pointed her toe down at the fish. "Walleye?"

The man nodded. He said, "Are you warm enough?" His voice was softer than she expected, coming from such a big frame. His teeth didn't look so good.

"I'll manage," Tracy said.

The man used his free hand to pull a big blue windbreaker-type garment from the duffel bag at his side, and he spread it on the ground next to him, invited her with a gesture to sit down. Tracy sat herself and pulled her knees in to her chest, held them there with her hands clasped in front of her. She pulled her coat sleeves down so they met her gloves at her wrist bones. It was cold. The full moon was white and textured like a biscuit, as though it might crumble to pieces if disturbed. The man cast an enormous shadow across the ice behind them.

An auger and a chisel rested on the ice next to her. She pointed to a tool with a thin screen, like some oversized kitchen apparatus.

"What's that?" she asked.

"Skimmer," the man said. "Scoops out the slush when you're making your hole."

"Ah-ha." Tracy observed that the man was using an early-model jigging rod with what looked to Tracy like monofilament fishing line; fancy stuff she'd learned from her dad. The stars were bright now. She identified both Dippers, then Orion, in the cloudless sky and pointed them out to the man.

"What kind of a jig have you got on there?" she asked.

"Grub," he said. He held up his fingers to indicate the length of it; about three inches.

"My dad used those," Tracy said.

The man lifted the rod then released several more feet of line into the hole.

"You live around here?" Tracy said.

The man seemed confused by the question, and she thought maybe he'd misheard. She decided to drop it. Water lapped quietly deep inside the hole. The man absently reeled in a few inches of his line. Tracy watched him for a minute or two. The moon cast soft blue all across the frozen lake.

"Would you let me have a go at that?" she said. "I've got a pretty good touch."

The man handed her the rod. The line felt taut and the pole was heavier than she expected. The grip was cork and had a nice softness in her left hand.

"Any secrets?" Tracy asked. "I know fishing but I've never done it in the ice."

"Fishing's fishing," the man said. "Just bounce her around a little bit every minute or two."

"You mind if I reel your jig in," she said, "just to see what I'm working with?"

The handle ticked peacefully in her hands as she reeled in the jig. She examined the bait up close. It was a pink and black speckled soft plastic grub body, slippery and lifelike, a two-color contrast eyeball. A hefty two-pronged hook protruded from the thing's chest.

Tracy admired the jig, then sent it back into the water, casting and releasing down what she imagined to be ten or twelve feet of line. It had been a while, but still she loved the weight of a fishing rod in her hands, her fingers trained and sensitive to every movement and vibration beneath the water. She wondered if the man was noticing how good her technique was.

"My dad had a good saying," she said. "'*The fishing was good; it was the catching that was bad.*'"

The man smiled.

"You know," Tracy continued, "I wish we could've fished more, me and my dad. He knew so much about it. But he was pretty much outta the picture," she explained, glancing at the man.

Tracy bounced the line and stared down into the hole for a moment.

Then she tipped her head back to look into the sky. "Hell of a moon tonight," she said. She tried to remember back to her night, before it had been shaken by the phone call. Something had woken her—was it the light of this moon? Was it a dream?

"Tonight I dreamed . . ." Tracy said, staring across the glittering frozen lake all the way to the downtown skyline, where the lights were tall stacks of unblinking gold eyeballs. "I dreamed I lived a different life."

Tracy pulled the line in and fingered the jig in her lap. She bent the two-pronged hook ever so slightly so that it was symmetrical, then sent it back into the hole.

The man pulled off his gloves and balanced them on his lap.

Then, he loosened the scarf around his neck, took one end in his hand, and he started to unwrap the scarf, circling it around his head.

"Why are you doing that?" she said.

The man didn't answer, but continued to unwrap his long scarf and he did it rhythmically, dipping his head, like this was a beautiful, slow dance that he had done many times before. Around and around he went with his left arm, gathering the long scarf in his right.

Tracy felt a pumping strangeness settle inside her, and her grip on the rod in her hands loosened; she let the line go slack.

The man reached the end of the scarf and pointed his chin up to the sky so that his whole neck was exposed. Tracy gasped. A grotesque tattoo of a snake circled his throat. Two inches thick and circling the whole way around his neck, scaled with blacks and deep greens. Tracy stared at the detailing at the front, directly over the man's Adam's apple. The serpent's mouth open, fangs dripping, preparing to devour its own tail.

Tracy recoiled. It was hideous. "What on earth . . ." She whispered.

The wind swirled around them in frosty spinning cones.

Tracy leaned in for a closer look at his tattoo. "Did it hurt?"

"Yes," he said.

Tracy continued to stare at the tattoo, the snake's jaw open wide and dripping, ravenous to destroy its own tail.

Tracy said, "I feel afraid."

"It's OK." The man nodded up into the sky and said, "Look there."

Tracy looked upward and was startled to see that the moon had gone red, glowing rusty like a big chunk of brick up there.

"What's happening?" she whispered.

"Lunar eclipse," the man said.

Tracy had never seen one before, not even on TV or anything. It was really remarkable. There was a gold arc developing over the northernmost edge of the moon. It looked like it had a pulse.

Tracy glanced up at the man, who rotated his toothpick back and forth in his lips. She didn't feel afraid anymore—just very peculiar.

She blinked up at that moon and suddenly remembered something.

"Do you know what? My dad used to sing a song to me, about a red moon." She tried to remember the words from the song, and caught the tail of a tune. She hummed half a line, before the memory dismantled.

"I had it but I lost it," she said. Her father had a funny, warbling singing voice. It was a senseless song about a red moon, maybe it was a red moon pie, she thought now, *Red moon pie, in the sky*, something like that, perhaps . . . She was having a hard time holding on to anything exact. She hummed something again. *Fly me up into the sky for a slice of that red moon pie* . . . Was that it? She bounced the fishing rod, reeled in a foot or two, and looked at the man. He didn't seem terribly interested in the red moon song, but he hadn't asked her to leave or quit yapping or give him back the rod or anything.

She thought for a minute, eyeing that red moon. Now she was honing in on the melody. A crinkled foil Cheetos bag skittered across the ice before them.

"I don't have a very good voice," she said, "but the tune went like this." She sang a little bit. "Do you know it?"

The man shook his head.

"*Damn*," she said. "I had the feeling you might. I sure wish I could remember the words." She hummed the tune again, then stopped and shrugged.

She was very cold now. The wind was picking up and her nose felt as though it was encased in ice. Her bottom was numb. She wished she had a camera on her to get a shot of the eclipse. Shelly might not believe her tomorrow, unless Shelly was out right now, seeing it for herself. What a strange galaxy this was. *Red moon pie, me oh my . . .*

"Sure wish I could remember the words to that song," Tracy said again. She had sung the red moon song to her mom at the end of that summer, when she was back home in Buffalo, but her mom didn't care for it too much.

She hummed it again.

"I like it," said the man.

Tracy laughed brightly. "I told you I don't have a very good voice."

"Sing it again?" the man said.

"Well, but I don't even know the *words*!" Tracy hummed the tune again and added in some round vowel noises at several points, tried to do a little vibrato. Maybe her singing voice was nicer than she thought.

Humming it through another time or two, she felt she was getting closer to some words. They were right there, those words, she could almost touch them. She just couldn't quite latch onto a phrase. She and her dad had sung it over and over that summer, when they were out at dusk, fishing for pike in the Lake Michigan channel off the dark cement pier that was streaked white with seagull poop. She couldn't believe she'd somehow misplaced those words in her memory; they were so simple. *Peeking down from my red moon pie . . .* Now what *was* it?

Tracy thought she felt a bite on the line, and she abruptly stopped singing as she twitched the pole to make the grub jump, far below. Then she was very still, waiting for another tug on the line. She stared down the hole, into that great deep black below them. She could scarcely believe there was life down there.

Who lives on a little red moon . . . Did somebody live on the red moon? Was that it? That wasn't quite right. She could smell the fish blood from the walleye at her side, it was hot and raw in her nostrils. The wind hissed over the ice.

What were those words? They were right there, just beyond her grasp. They kept dissolving every time she thought she'd nabbed them. *What were those words?*

She stared out across the frozen lake and it looked like alien land, gray and pocked and gleaming.

"My dad was an all right guy," she said.

WHITE MORNING LIGHT

The Christmas morning sun split the day wide open like a cracked egg over the cold, clean horizon. White morning light soared in through the windows. Something in this world felt different to Tracy. As though everything that had come before was part of a different dream.

Tracy gazed at her stack of presents for Shelly's family and pictured Shelly's home, where the kids would probably wake soon to rip through their presents under the tree. She hoped she hadn't overlapped on any presents that Shelly and Mac had already gotten the kids. She probably should've checked that, it occurred to her now, although it would have ruined the surprise. Tracy pictured Shelly waking to remove her sleep mask and ear plugs—she'd always been a light sleeper. She pictured Mr. and Mrs. Green, who were probably still sleeping now, in their queen-size bed with pale pink sheets. The one night Tracy had spent at their place, when Mr. and Mrs. Green were out of town, she and Greenie had slept in their queen-size bed, since his was a twin. Their sheets smelled of baby powder and dandruff shampoo and vaguely of curry. There was a jar of petroleum jelly and an issue of *Reader's Digest* on the bed stand. Tracy tried to picture Greenie now, imagining where he might wake on this Christmas morning, but he felt so far away she could barely even pin down his sleeping face in her mind. She pictured the ice fisherman from just an hour or two before. She wondered what somebody like that did for Christmas—she couldn't believe she hadn't thought to ask. She pictured the ladies of Paxico, Kansas, waking to small jewelry boxes from their husbands placed under Christmas trees or in stockings. She pictured her father bent over and hard at work on the pieces, painstakingly winding small parts together. Tracy had about a dozen pairs of earrings currently on display at La-Di-Da, and although they weren't fetching the same prices that Bruce Lemon had offered, she still thought it important to insert herself in the local market. She also planned to finally take Shelly up on her offer to secure Tracy a booth at the Bella Vista Arts & Crafts Fair, which would be held in Rochester, in March.

Tracy pictured a tiny version of herself, in this very room on Christmas morning 1983, the last Christmas she ever spent with her father, and at this memory she was walloped by something that was not entirely painless, but thunderously powerful and acute. 1983, when these carpets were thick and rust-colored, the curtains flowered, the television set a small rabbit-eared black box. Details were knocking against one another in the very softest part of her. Was this nostalgia? Love? Was there a difference?

Could she recall this warm memory with such intense particularity if there was not also the same measure of love attached? 1983, when her father wore a red flannel shirt over a red cotton turtleneck and he drank black coffee. What she felt now was so pure, it was as though every emotion she'd ever had toward him had been distilled into this one moment, and the pained and joyous throbbing inside her almost felt like the beating of wings. 1983, when she knew nothing of the ways people fail each other; when she believed her father to be the best father.

It had all changed, she thought now, and she felt a deeply, wonderfully sad happiness at this. It had all changed, and it would all change again.

Several months later, Tracy would move into the little pink ranch home down the street, and several months after that, she would acquire her passport in order to retrieve her father's forty-pound muskie.

Before making the trip, Tracy first called the taxidermist in Wawa, Ontario, to confirm that the tiger muskie was still there. The taxidermist, now in his eighties, but the same guy who'd worked on the fish all those years ago, assured Tracy that the fish was not only there, but it was still in great shape.

The taxidermist warned Tracy that it wasn't the *prettiest* fish you'd ever see, and he asked Tracy what she knew about muskies. He explained that the name "muskie," from "muskellange," had its origins in the Ojibwa language: "Maashkinoozhe," meaning "ugly pike," because of its underbite. Nevertheless, the guy said, he'd grown fond of that ugly old thing and to this day it was displayed front and center inside his shop. He told Tracy that as much as he'd enjoyed having that tiger muskie around for all these years, he'd be delighted to return it to its rightful owner. Tracy consulted a lawyer who was an expert on customs regulations and filled out the necessary paperwork, requiring many signatures and a great deal of information about Marty; all his residences since the time the fish was caught, dates and registration numbers on his fishing and hunting licenses.

She finally got the green light from the customs officer assigned to the case and was told that the tiger muskie could be picked up from the taxidermy office in Wawa, Ontario, where it had lived for all these years, and she was guaranteed safe passage at the Sault Ste. Marie border crossing. The customs officer provided a case number and his own contact information for Tracy to reference at the border if they gave her any trouble. She didn't end up needing this—they waved her through with no questions.

The fish itself was hideous and magnificent. Its scales were waxy and gleaming, the deep green striping darkest at the flank, above a silvery beige. Its fins were stiff with glue but still delicate-looking, an iridescent orange. Its open-mouthed underbite was pronounced, and wide like a duckbill. Sharklike layers of needle-sharp teeth were exposed, circling a rubbery pink tongue. In its face, the thing looked more like a dragon than a fish. Its golden glass eyes had enlarged black pupils.

A plaque beneath the fish read:

40-Lb. Female Tiger Muskie
Lake Superior, 1977
Martin C. Calhoun

Tracy would hang the fish on the south wall of her living room, and sometimes she would try to imagine what it must have been like for her father to catch a fish of this size. He was a fairly slight man, and Tracy considered how forty pounds must have felt at the other end of Marty's pole.

Sometimes, Tracy ran a finger along the spiny dorsal fin of the muskie and imagined how this fin must have contracted like an accordion and splayed, slapping at the tiger muskie's sides, fighting to gain purchase as she realized she'd been ensnared. How the tiger muskie must have fought, how she must have raged. Tracy imagined how her gills must have chugged, her tail whipped mightily, this ugly mouth snapped and her eyeballs flared bright gold, rolling like planets on an axis. All that fight, that fury, that muscular force.

Tracy imagined how, rising from the water, the muskie must have continued to fight, jerking back and forth in her middle, even as hot oxygen assaulted her gills. Seeing the world above water for perhaps the first time; knowing, until that moment, nothing of its existence.

Tracy imagined that even after the tiger muskie had been slapped hard across the deck of the boat, her cheek torn and dripping cold blood, gills fluttering, even then, that tiger muskie kept fighting. Tracy imagined that the muskie's golden eyes bulged and raged, finally fixing upon the face of her captor, and she wondered if the maashkinoozhe paused for one moment to take notice of this, or if, with the last of her strength, she thrashed.

On the south wall of Tracy's new little pink ranch home, the fish would catch the light of the large west-facing windows from the hours of three o'clock in the afternoon until sunset. This wall would already, upon Tracy moving into the home, be painted a deep oceanic blue that would nicely frame and offset the colors of the fish. The fish would be positioned in the center of the wall and facing right so that it stared directly out the window, those golden eyes fixed on the sliver of gray shivering lake that could be seen between the neighbors' homes. Everyone who entered the house would comment on the fish, noticing how bright the colors became in the evening sun, and many would comment on what a *perfect place* this was for the fish, between the sunlight and the color of the wall and even the way that the fish had been mounted on wood that seemed to perfectly match the floorboards of this room.

It was, in fact, *such* a perfect place for the fish that it was almost like the little pink ranch home had been designed specifically for the very purpose of housing and displaying this very fish, back in the 1950s, when the home was first built. It was as if perhaps everything had always belonged this way, even before any of it came to life, or came to pass.

ACKNOWLEDGMENTS

Many of the themes explored in this book are inspired by Ojibwa culture. I am awed by the beauty and richness of the language, stories and spirituality, and hope I have properly conveyed the deepest respect.

For love, encouragement, and steadfastness, thank you to my family, Mom & Dad, Sissy, Mike, Cole, Pat, Jessie, and Andy, who we miss every day. Julie Buntin, dear and thoughtful reader, thank you for the time you spent with this book, and for your friendship. Thank you to the various communities that have lifted and supported me over the years, including the crew at LC&GH, where I laugh every day. Thank you to my agent, Michelle Tessler, for your unwavering belief in this book and guidance through many edits. Thank you Jack Shoemaker, Megan Fishmann, Kelly Winton, Joe Goodale, Ryan Quinn, Neuwirth & Associates, and the rest of the team at Counterpoint, for your vision and enthusiasm. Lastly, George, for your indomitable spirit, your gentleness, your constancy, and the joy and hilarity you bring to my daily life, I love you and thank you.

Printed in the United States
by Baker & Taylor Publisher Services